"Midnight might be the bewitching hour, but *11:59* is a coming-of-age thriller that will bewitch the reader for hours and days and weeks, long after finishing its last page"

—Parris Afton Bonds, New York Times Bestselling Author

"A young man learns that need, desire, and intellect fail to fill an empty, searching heart the way love and forgiveness can. The reader will find himself invested in Jackson's travels—and travails—through life."

—K.D. McCrite, Award Winning Author

"Every action has consequences, but most of those consequences you only understand in retrospect. *11:59* looks at how a chain of cause-and-effect going back decades leads one man to a place he'd never thought he'd be—and causes ripples that change the lives of everyone he knows."

—Gordon Bonnet, Author of *Descent Into Ulthoa*

"John Lennon said that life is what happens while you're busy making other plans. *11:59* follows one man's rise to the top, only to have life twist in a way he—and the reader—never expect. Jackson lulls you into his life slowly, grabs on tightly, and keeps you holding your breath with anticipation to the very last page."

—Gil Miller, Author of *The Rural Empires* Series

# 11:59

## MARLON HAYES

Text copyright © 2022 by Marlon Hayes
All Rights Reserved. Printed in the United States of America

Published by Motina Books, LLC, Van Alstyne, Texas
www.MotinaBooks.com

Library of Congress Cataloguing-in-Publication Data:

Names: Hayes, Marlon
Title: 11:59
Description: First Edition. | Van Alstyne: Motina Books, 2022

Identifiers:
LCCN: 2022942327

ISBN-13: 978-1-945060-67-0 (paperback)
ISBN-13: 978-1-945060-64-9 (e-book)
ISBN-13: 978-1-945060-66-3 (hardcover)

Subjects: BISAC:
FICTION / African American & Black / General

Cover Design: Diane Windsor
Interior Design: Diane Windsor

## Dedication

This book is dedicated to my wife, Traci Lynn Hayes (aka What's-Her-Name), who refused to let me quit on this novel. I love and appreciate you.

Also, to my mother, Sheila Hayes-Smiley, for teaching me to love words and stories. Sorry Ma, I would have been a terrible lawyer or doctor.

# 1

# 11:59:00

How long is a minute? Really, has anyone ever thought about it, or does everyone automatically respond, "Sixty seconds?" For some, a minute can seem to drag on forever. For others, a minute is so brief it's as short as an exhaled breath. My story, to me, will only take about a minute or so, but it may seem like an eon to others, who may not possess the valuable gift of patience.

The clock on the wall currently reads 11:59:00. It's all I've been staring at for the last three minutes or so. I'm recalling all of the seconds, minutes, and hours I've wasted in my life. I lament the time squandered on climbing the social ladder or chasing financial daydreams.

Only now do I realize I'm going to leave here the same way I came in, naked and broke. All the money in the world can't save any of us from the increasingly louder footsteps of the Grim Reaper, who is still undefeated.

The downfall of the typical male in history has not been for a cause or because of misguided ideals. No, the typical male is usually felled by the same demon which cast Adam from the garden of Eden. Women. For most of my life, I prided myself as an atypical male, immune to the disease of women which has beheaded so many of my brethren ever since Adam bit the apple. Nothing happens overnight, not in life anyway. There's a gradual slide to the hell we create for ourselves, but we're usually blinded by our own sense of invincibility. At the end of everything, I'm still only a man.

Her face, her body, and her voice are etched into the walls around my heart and soul. The great love affair books and movies promise us wasn't my Holy Grail. Not even close. My pursuits lie in other directions until she walked, or rather, sashayed into my life. Nora, beautiful Nora of the killer curves and the sultry voice. My Nora, the most alluring creature I've ever laid my eyes upon. Nora was my Helen of Troy, my Delilah, and my Bonnie Parker, all encapsulated in one package.

Thirty or so years ago, in the Mississippi Delta, I was born to the union of Raymond and Flora Jean Jackson, a young married Black couple. I'm reiterating Black to point out the difference between my existence and the existence of my white contemporaries. I know that most people north of the Mason-Dixon line don't understand the reality of the two Mississippis, one white, one dark. I was born into a system not designed for me to succeed because I wasn't the right color. Mississippi is the part of America folks don't like to talk about, acknowledge, not to each other, and especially not with company.

My mama, Flora Jean, was the cook, maid, and nurse for the Fitzgerald family, the richest white family in our region of Mississippi. In the mornings before the cock crowed, she and I would trudge down the road to my grandmother's house, where I'd be left to spend the day until she returned. My mama's day didn't end until after she'd served dinner to old Mr. Fitzgerald and his wife. I bet the Fitzgeralds never realized how integral my mother was to their everyday existence. Breakfast, lunch, dinner, dusting, ironing, cleaning, polishing, and performing whatever service was required. The welfare of her own family was not the concern of the people she worked for. It was up to Flora Jean to take care of her family, even though she worked five days every week, and sometimes weekends, depending on if the Fitzgeralds were entertaining guests or not.

My father, Raymond, was a solitary, gruff man who only came to life a little bit when he'd been drinking. He was either working or drinking, that was it. As I got older, I tried to see what could have possibly sparked my mother's interest. He wasn't loquacious, charming, or even remotely attractive. He was a big man, dark as charcoal, with few redeeming qualities. In the time I knew him we never had a warm, familial relationship. The communication between Raymond and me consisted of him giving me an order, and me complying with his request. That was basically it. There wasn't ever a question from him inquiring how my school day was, or if I was hungry, or even if the fish were biting. I never called him by any term of endearment, not Dad, Pop, or even Raymond. When I was forced by circumstances to address him, I'd either call him sir, or leave my question open ended with no form of address.

Flora Jean on the other hand, was bubbling over with life. Pecan-colored, with a beautiful singing voice, and the gift to always make me feel better about myself or any situation. On our morning walk to my grandmother's, we'd talk about books, movies, music, and anything else which crossed her mind. Once I started attending school daily, we'd still walk to my grandma's, and the school bus would pick me up there, and drop me off there after school. Those morning walks were so important to my view of the world and my place in it. She stressed to me I was Black, but not to let my skin color ever be a handicap or a crutch. Being born Black wasn't a curse, but it was a long time before I realized it.

"But if it's not a curse, then why do white folks treat us so bad for being Black?" I asked. "White women clutch they purses when I go past, and I ain't big enough to scare nobody, Mama."

"Use your good English, baby," she replied, admonishing me for using "they" instead of "their."

She started singing a hymn, as was her way, and I joined in, enjoying the moment and the sweet sound of my mother's voice. I didn't realize until later she never answered my question.

My mother spent her off days with me, taking me to the library on Saturday afternoons, then for an ice cream at the parlor in town. Our little blue house was about a mile outside of town, and Raymond had a ratty old pickup truck. He never took us anyplace in that crappy vehicle. This meant Flora Jean and I walked everywhere, which gave her the opportunity to point out the beauty of nature. The Mississippi Delta has so much to offer as far as flora and fauna are concerned. Even the fields of cotton appeal to the eye as something wondrous until you think of the blood and toil which went into making cotton King. Knowing the history of cotton tainted its beauty in my eyes.

There were magnolias, shortleaf pines, oak, elm, willow, aspen, bald cypress, walnut, ash, and hickory trees. Some of them were tall and vigorous, and others were gnarled and bent, as if they had survived hundreds of years of storms, which they probably had. I looked at the trees of the Delta, and I felt small and young. I imagined the things those sentient trees had witnessed and I shuddered, because even as a young boy, I knew some of the dark history of where I lived.

Flora Jean taught me to love books, but my Grandma Lily was who taught me how to read. She was my daily caregiver and teacher until I was twelve. My grandma trained me to recite and learn my letters as a toddler, rewarding my efforts with treats for getting the cadence of the ABC song correct. Dr. Seuss was the first author I can remember with certainty, but due to my grandma, I became a voracious reader, a characteristic which I would carry with me for my entire life. My grandma's encyclopedia set was a treasure to me, in the years before the Internet explosion. The weekly trips to the library with my mama were the highlight of my week, as I fell in love with Ramona and Beezus, the Pevensie children, Mr. Baggins, and all of the other fictional characters which enrich one's childhood.

My grandma also taught me how to fish, in the creek not too far from her house. The creek was on her property, so we didn't have far to go. Lily was only in her fifties when I was a boy, still spry and active enough to teach a young boy to love the tranquility of time spent fishing. She'd be waiting for my mother to drop me off, with her tackle box and rods ready to go. The bait we used depended on whatever she'd cooked for dinner the night before. We used shrimp, chicken, small pieces of pork, and catfish. The use of catfish as bait seemed so cannibalistic to me, because we used catfish to catch their brethren. I know catfish really don't care what they eat, but it gave me the creeps as a young boy, as if I was baiting a fish with the carcass of its brother. Childish, I know, but think about it.

I learned which fish we could eat, and which ones to throw back into the creek. The small ones were a no-brainer, and at first I couldn't understand why she would throw back some of the larger catfish, which probably weighed twenty pounds or more.

"Them big ones is old," she explained. "They old, evil, and tough, because they done made it a long time eating everything they can, and they meat is disgusting. We only want the young, plump ones. We can fry 'em up, or grill 'em, and they just as tender as can be. Don't nobody want no old catfish."

Looking back now, I think my grandma was the

smartest and funniest woman I ever met. Her views on life kept me thinking, observing, and laughing. She told me early on, there was no real difference between white people and Black people. "See baby, Black folks know they ain't no differences between us and them," she explained. "But white folks wanna think they somethin' special. They wanna claim everything, like they was the first ones to create something, but everything they love, from fried food to barbecue to they music, they stole or learned from us. Naw, they ain't nothing special."

She was full of humorous anecdotes, stories, and old sayings, some of which I thought she invented herself like, "God-willing and da' creek don't rise," or "You eva wonder who thought it would be good to suck on a cow's breast for milk?" My grandma was my best friend and the person I spent the most time with. I treasure those moments now because those memories are all I have of her.

Going to school was both a gift and a curse. I loved learning of new places, reading books, the history of America, and figuring out solutions to problems. The social aspects of school disappointed me, leaving me disenchanted, disillusioned, and disgusted. Mississippi wasn't legally segregating the schools, but they weren't exactly breaking down walls to support integration. My school was an all Black school, the student body consisting of children living within ten miles of the town. Yes, everyone was Black, but being Black is not necessarily a unifier. Different financial backgrounds, differences in how the children were being raised, and different complexions.

Yes, different complexions. Non-Blacks don't realize the self hating scars which slavery has afflicted Black people with. During slavery there were slave owners who raped or cajoled their female slaves into sex, resulting in children who were way more light-skinned than their forebears. Due to the white people's theory they were superior; lighter-skinned slaves were thought to be smarter or more attractive, due to their complexion. Lighter-skinned slaves more often than not worked in the "Big House," whereas darker-skinned slaves worked the fields, picking cotton until they dropped. The system of pitting slaves against each other based on skin complexion is a curse which has survived in America until this very day. If proof is necessary, look at the movies, television, or popular magazines. Were Lena Horne and Dorothy Dandridge more talented than Pearl Bailey or Juanita Moore? Or were they seen as prettier because they were light-skinned? The caste system still exists.

I learned of the differences between my classmates and me within the first couple of weeks of school. I was asked by a couple of classmates if I were white, then the giggles and name calling started after I assured them I was Black. I was the lightest boy amongst my classmates by far, causing them to shun me, tease me, and some even attempted to bully me. I fought every bully, returned every insult hurled at me, and I became a loner due to circumstance, not by choice. I didn't raise my hand to answer questions in class because if I did, it would draw attention to me. Nor did I go out of my way to be friendly towards any of my classmates. They made a loner out of me, making me enjoy my own company, which became my *modus operandi* throughout my life. Sure, I'd have loved to have at least one friend of my own age during my childhood, but it never happened. Children are cruel creatures, yet their behavior is learned from adults.

From an objective point of view, my childhood was routine and mostly satisfying. I fished with my grandma, talked with my mama, and devoured every book I could. One blemish on my childhood was the strange and strained relationship I had with my father, Raymond. Our conversations were either a question or a command, responded to with a one-word answer, or an instant action. It was a little bizarre, but I had nothing with which to compare our relationship. No friends or cousins with whom to make comparisons and the fathers on television were totally unrealistic to me, considering my own situation. I didn't dwell on the strangeness of our relationship until later on down the line, when everything became clear to me.

Not having any friends made me quite industrious as a boy. My mama bought me a bike when I was nine, and that bike allowed me the freedom of movement I needed. By the time I was eleven, I had a job delivering newspapers on my bicycle before school. After school, I'd use the bike to deliver groceries. I learned the value of money, because when a person has money, all things are possible. Or at least I thought they were for most of my life. I could afford to do things which my classmates couldn't, such as buy an ice cream when I wanted, or go to the movies. It would have been great to have a pal to go to the show with, and I'd even have paid for them. I had no one but myself. I always saved half of my earnings for a rainy day, because life can change in an instant, and one always has to be prepared.

# 2

# 11:59:05

In my life, I realize most of the events which took place were beyond my control. The few things I did control didn't always go the way I'd planned. Being unprepared for eventualities seems to be the human Achilles heel, always fucking us up at the wrong time. Whenever we think we have shit under control, the other shoe drops, blowing away all of our plans. Each event in our lives relates to the next event. I think of it as a domino effect of shit storms, guiding us down unfamiliar and unwanted paths. It's a sad and frustrating acknowledgement to realize in the chess game of life—one has only ever been a pawn, never a more meaningful or powerful

11

piece. I always tried to remain upbeat and positive, but life has a way of bringing out our cynicism, despite our best efforts.

Summertime always began for me with the last day of school. The last bell of that blessed day was a knell to the freedom which summertime promised. Lazy days of fishing and reading, riding my bike down country roads, hanging out on my grandma's porch until my mama came, and not having to deal with the scorn and disdain of my classmates.

The summer I turned thirteen, I learned of the domino effect of life. Two days after I'd been paroled from school, Old Man Fitzgerald passed away from a sudden heart attack. The town and surrounding areas reacted as if the governor had died. Flags were flown at half mast, the newspaper dedicated almost the whole paper to eulogizing him, and Bobby Fitzgerald Jr. came home.

The town where I was raised could have changed its name to Fitzgerald, and no one would have batted an eye. The lumber mill, the paper mill, and plenty of land in the area were owned by the Fitzgeralds. The entire region had been under the thumb of the Fitzgerald family since the early 1950s, and it seemed it would always be.

Bobby Fitzgerald Jr. was a mythical creature, rarely seen by the townspeople, maybe once or twice a year, around Christmas or the Fourth of July. He was the only child, the Golden Boy who'd led the high school to a state championship in football, the only sport which mattered in the South. He'd matriculated to the university in Starkville, adding even more accolades to his impeccable public resume. After graduation he'd attended law school, and then married the most sought after debutante in Mississippi. People wondered why he never ran for public office, because he'd have been a shoo-in for any office he'd want. Instead, he ran his family's businesses from an office up in Memphis.

The return of Bobby "The Golden Boy" Fitzgerald Jr. increased my mother's workload significantly. The Fitzgerald household had doubled, because not only was there Old Lady Fitzgerald, but also the Golden Boy's two children. The previous year his wife and he had divorced, amicably according to the newspapers, yet he had sole custody of his children, a girl of around my age, Susanna, and a boy, Bobby Fitzgerald III. If the divorce had been so amicable, then why was the ex-wife not in the picture anymore, as any other mother would be? Simple, because the Fitzgeralds didn't want to share, and as I found out, they always got what they wanted.

My mother would leave around five in the morning Monday through Friday, and I wouldn't see her again until after supper time. She never complained or lamented, because she wasn't the type of woman to ever complain. When she'd come to get me from Grandma's the three of us would eat dinner together, talking and laughing until long after dark. Then Flora Jean and I would walk home in the darkness, talking and singing as we went. My mother's voice was so beautiful, it seemed as if the crickets and other night creatures paused in their noisemaking, just to listen to her.

"Mama, why do you sing so much?" I asked, on one of our nightly walks. "Most people here only sing in church."

"I sing to keep myself to me," she said. "I have thoughts and feelings and emotions that wouldn't be mine anymore if I told the world how I feel about things. But if I sing a song of love, or praise, or even a blues song, I'm expressing my feelings without ever saying a word to anybody. If you listen, then you can read what's on my heart. It's our secret, okay?"

I nodded as she looked at me, kind of understanding. She smiled at me in the darkness, and then started singing a gospel song—*I'll Fly Away*. I clasped her hand in mine, even though I was no longer a little boy.

My summer routine was simple. I'd leave around 6 A.M. to walk to the newspaper office, where I'd pick up my bundle of newspapers. I'd have all of my newspapers delivered before nine, at which time I'd go to the grocery store. Back then, there were customers who had accounts with the grocery store. They'd phone the grocer their orders, and I'd deliver them on my bicycle with the wagon attached. It was easy work for me, and I'd receive a tip from most of the customers because my efforts kept them from having to venture out into the sweltering Mississippi afternoons.

Around one I'd be finished for the day, so I'd either ride to the library or go fishing in the creek behind Grandma's house. Fish never seemed to really bite in the afternoon as much as they did at daybreak. Probably due to the heat of the Mississippi sun. I'd still go though, armed with a book, my rod, some bait, and a little cooler filled with cold drinks. My routine never varied much, because it wasn't as if I had friends to hang out with, or a baseball game to play or watch. All of my friends were located in the books I read, which was just fine with me. After fishing, usually unsuccessfully, I'd park my bike at my grandma's house to spend the rest of the day with her.

On one particular Tuesday I'd skipped fishing, opting instead for the library. I'd recently became intrigued with Alexander Dumas, a French writer whom I'd discovered was Black. Or at least Black by American standards which meant a person was Black if any of their recent ancestors had a trace of Africa in their DNA. *The Count of Monte Cristo* was my choice to get me started on the works of Dumas, and I looked forward to discussing the book and its author with my grandma.

I parked my bike alongside her front porch, hearing the faint sound of the blues coming from Grandma's kitchen radio. I opened the screen door and saw she was taking a nap in her favorite easy chair. Just as quietly as I'd entered I exited with the same manner, making sure not to let the screen door slam. I'd let her nap for awhile, then I'd wake her later so I could help with cooking dinner. I settled myself onto the front porch swing, accompanied by my cooler of cold drinks. I opened up my book and became totally engrossed in the tale of Edmond Dantès.

I guess I hadn't realized how much time had passed, because the footsteps and voice of my mama snapped me out of my reverie. She'd gotten off a little early and walked to my grandma's. The sun was almost in the west, so it must've been around six in the evening. When she inquired about Grandma, I informed her she had been asleep when I'd arrived and I hadn't attempted to wake her. After my statement my mother and I entered the house together, both of us seeing she was still asleep. My mother leaned over my grandma and whispered, "Mama." When my grandma didn't immediately wake up, my mother began to nudge her gently, still calling her name. "Mama?" she said, beginning to shake my grandma more vigorously, but to no avail. Her eyes remained closed, and I touched her hand. It was cold. She would never take me fishing again, or listen to my stories. She was gone.

The ambulance that carried my grandma away never even turned its siren on. There was no need to. Grandma had already departed for Eternity, long before my mother had attempted to wake her. She died peacefully (How does anyone know?) in her sleep, according to the county coroner, of a heart attack. The coroner attempted to console us by telling us of the myth about God calling His most faithful servants into Eternity while they slept, waking them only so they could witness the beauty of Heaven. Whatever. My heart took no solace from his attempts, and I realized then when people have suffered a loss, it's best to simply pat them on the back or give a hug, while mumbling condolences. Platitudes such as *she's in a better place* are worthless and ignorant. How does anyone know if where she's gone is a better place? Are there catfish there? Or music? Or anything?

Raymond never showed at the hospital, nor did he show up at back at our house. Neighbors, church members, and other well-wishers stopped by, dropping off casseroles, pies, cakes, and good intentions. Raymond wasn't even missed by anyone, because no one inquired about him. His wife didn't even seem to miss him. He was a pathetic, angry man, with little human emotion within him. I found it difficult then to understand what had made him and my mother become a couple. It was a mystery because they were as different in demeanor and character as a dove and a bull.

After all of the well-wishers had gone on their way, the emotional dam broke for the two of us. We'd remained stoic while company was present, simply hugging neighbors and saying "thank you." Once they left, Mama and I sat on the couch the entire night, holding each other and sobbing. Eventually, we fell into sleep on the couch due to utter emotional exhaustion.

It seemed to me as if my mother awoke the next morning refreshed and full of resolve. She became a whirlwind from then on, handling everything the world confronted her with. The morning after my grandma's death, Flora Jean skillfully and willfully arranged the funeral, the burial, and the repast. She was flexible with the funeral arrangements. The only thing she was adamant about was the lilies. She demanded that lilies be festooned around the church in celebration of Grandma Lily, the most beautiful lily which had ever existed.

We trudged along the rest of the week, bracing ourselves for the funeral. We still went to work, though, if only to have a routine to keep us from dwelling on our grief. Staying busy helps with grief a little, but a funeral always brings it back. I delivered my papers and the groceries as usual, then I'd return to our house, where I'd nap and read until my mother came home. My mother diligently took care of the Fitzgeralds, and Raymond did his usual. He went to work at the paper mill, staying away as much as possible. If he wasn't at work, he could be

17

found down at the juke joint, drinking heavily with his cronies. He would come home late at night after we were already asleep, leaving again early in the morning, soon after sunrise.

The Saturday of my grandma's funeral was a sunny, sultry, and sticky kind of morning, one of those days when it feels as if one is being barbecued or slow-roasted in an oven. Add mourning clothes to weather resembling hell's front porch, and a person is a sweating, soggy mess by noon. My mother and I walked to the church slowly, holding hands as we walked. Raymond drove by us as we were nearing the church, and I spent a brief moment trying to recall if I'd ever been in his truck. Never, not one time in my life.

The small old church was filled to capacity with calla lilies everywhere. Every Black person within twenty miles was there to celebrate my grandma's life. The songs uplifted the congregation, while the sermons evoked tears and cries of "Amen" from the mourners. Lily had been a much-loved member of her church family and the community as a whole. It's sad but true—none of us really think about the effects our grandparents or parents have on other people. The selfishness of ownership is ingrained so deeply, we only think of our parents and grandparents as appendages of us, not realizing they have their own lives. She lived an entirely separate life apart from being Flora Jean's mom, or my grandmother. She went to school there, worked with some of these folks, or knew them from church or the grocery store or the tackle shop. I would not be the only person grieving her.

The funeral procession was typically sad, and salty

water flowed constantly from my eyes. As her casket descended into the grave, the finality of the situation hit me. I'd no longer go fishing with my grandma, nor would I ever again be hugged by her as if I were the most precious gift from God. My accomplishments wouldn't be applauded by her, and her own dreams for the rest of her life were forever aborted. I understood, finally, what death really meant. Death wasn't peaceful sleep or rest, it was the blank screen at the end of the movie.

The repast consisted of food, laughter, the regaling of stories starring my grandma, and the flow of liquor. A repast is a party to celebrate the life of the departed, as well as to give hope to the mourners of better days ahead. I sat back, observing everyone, especially my parents. While Flora Jean moved around the room, hugging people, laughing, and having the occasional drink, Raymond sat in the corner by himself, accompanied only by an ever shrinking bottle of whiskey. He'd occasionally nod at someone, or briefly shake hands, but he didn't share in any merrymaking or conversation. After a couple of hours, at the height of the party, Raymond simply slunk out the side door, an unwanted guest as far as I was concerned, one who would not be missed.

After the final "goodbyes" were uttered and after the final hugs with the mourners, my mama and I started to walk home. There had been offers of transportation, which we'd declined. There was comfort in the holding of hands as we slowly walked. This was our routine, and I pretended in my head we were only walking from my grandma's house, just like any other night.

"Things will be different going forward, Robby," my

mother said, her voice sounding tired. "I know you're growing up, and soon you'll start questioning the things happening around you. Pay attention to things you hear and see, and try to keep your feelings to yourself. If no one knows what you're thinking or feeling, no one will have the power to hurt you. Okay?"

"I do have one question," I said, a slight grin making me feel a little better. "When are you going to stop calling me Robby? If I'm becoming more mature, shouldn't you start calling me Rob or Robert? Might as well get used to the idea, Ma."

She wrapped her arm around my shoulder, and out of the corner of my eye, I saw her smiling. At that moment, I felt as if everything was going to be all right. Lily was gone, but she had put enough good stuff in me that I would be able to move forward with my life, without her. My mother was going to be all right as well, because she was the daughter of a great woman. Lily used to say that the key to making it through dark spots in life was to remember the sun will always shine through. I looked up at the heavens, feeling reassured because I knew Lily was up there looking out for me. I vowed to make her proud.

Suddenly, the quiet summer night was ripped apart by the sounds of wailing sirens and the acrid aroma of smoke. The smoke was billowing through the air, grayish black, made even more visible by the lights of the sirens. Fitzgerald's paper mill, which employed at least two hundred men including Raymond, burned completely to the ground that night, leaving all of those men unemployed. The dominoes just kept falling.

# 3

# 11:59:09

I'm sitting here stuffed full of food, awash in memories which normally would have taken my appetite away. Maybe the excellence of my recently decimated meal overcame my reticence in recalling difficult and painful memories. Prime rib, medium well, a twice-baked potato, dinner rolls, creamed spinach, and I even managed to eat dessert, key lime pie. My meal was excellent in all aspects, now I just needed it to settle down in my churning stomach. It would be a shame if such a wondrous meal couldn't stay down.

The morning after my grandma's funeral, the acrid smell of smoke from the paper mill permeated the region.

It had been a huge factory, and the firefighters from the neighboring towns were still at the scene, making sure that the burning coals didn't spread to other buildings near it. Raymond was now out of work, which wouldn't bode well for our already contentious familial relationship. Raymond used to be just a weekend drinker, getting sloshed before and during football games. He rarely worked weekend shifts, preferring to sleep in or use his ratty pickup truck to collect scrap to either fix or sell. He'd normally start his drinking around 11 A.M., during the pregame telecast. Cheap whiskey and beer would fuel him usually until around 4 P.M. at which time he'd either pass out where he sat, or get in his truck and leave. He wasn't what I'd consider an angry drunk, he just sank deeper and deeper into himself, unwittingly teaching me the definition of the word, *morose.*

As we sat at our kitchen table the morning after my grandma's funeral, my mother told me of my inheritance. The property we lived on, as well as my grandma's, would belong to me if my mother preceded me in death. Flora Jean said that we'd rent out my grandma's house, using the income derived from it to pay the property taxes. All other profits would be put into a trust for me until I turned eighteen. I could then use the money for college or whatever I wanted to with it.

"What about Raymond?" I asked.

"It's not his property nor his business, so he's of no concern in this," she said.

I should have taken advantage of the moment to ask my mama the questions which had burned in me for as long as I could remember. Such as how she and Raymond came to be a couple, because I'd never witnessed any kind of closeness or emotional connection between them. I should have asked how she'd started working for the Fitzgeralds and why she still worked for them. From what I knew of my mother, she was well-read, an excellent cook, and was skilled and diligent with her hands. She could have worked anywhere, yet she chose to continue at the Fitzgeralds. But I elected not to ask. I had been raised to not question grown-ups, no matter what. Plus, I figured I had plenty of time to find out all of the answers.

The following Monday, my new routine started. Or rather *our* new routine started. My mama left at daybreak, and I would leave for my jobs soon after. Raymond would go on his scrap metal missions, finishing his day around noon when his drinking would start. Not having a set work schedule gave Raymond the freedom to get as drunk as he wanted to on a daily basis. By the end of July, I'd overheard he and my mother arguing about his drinking more than once.

Maybe the final straw for Flora Jean was when Raymond, while driving drunk, crashed his truck into someone's barn. He wasn't hurt, not even a scratch, but his truck was completely totaled and he had to pay for the damaged barn out of his own money. My mother refused to help him pay for the barn, further widening the rift between them. By the beginning of August they were no longer sharing a bedroom, nor were they speaking to one another. My mama went to the Fitzgeralds every day now, not just the weekdays. I did my best to stay out of the house as much as I could, working, fishing, riding my bike, or reading a book under a tree somewhere. I could've used a friend during that period, but not having any, I suffered alone.

My birthday was approaching, August fifteenth. My mama was taking the day off so we could spend my thirteenth birthday together. I wanted to go to Memphis for the day, because I'd never been. There was an amusement park there, another place I'd never been. Flora Jean had arranged for transportation there and back with a neighbor of ours. She'd pay for his gas and lodging, and I'd be able to finally ride a roller coaster. As the date got nearer, I was giddy with an excitement I'd never felt before, as if I were on the precipice of a great and memorable adventure. It would be my first time leaving the state of Mississippi, something I'd dreamt of daily.

On August fourteenth I woke at my usual time, hurrying out of the house in an effort to speed the day along. I pedaled my bike furiously, finishing my newspaper deliveries in half my usual time. My grocery deliveries were delivered in a fast but careful manner, because I didn't want to smash anyone's eggs. I was in a hurry, but not to the extent I couldn't perform my job in an excellent and efficient manner.

I skipped fishing for a change, and went straight home after I finished my deliveries. Memphis was beckoning and I wanted to be well-rested. I was still muscling through Dumas, enjoying it immensely. I was currently reading about D'Artagnan and his fateful trip to Paris on an ugly yellow horse.

It was another blisteringly hot Mississippi day. The heat was unbearable in the sun, but I knew it would be cool enough in the house. Our air conditioning unit was centrally located in our living room, allowing for cool air to be dispersed throughout the house. I put my bike away and opened up the front door, and let the air conditioning welcome me home.

Raymond was sitting in our living room polishing the shotgun he used for hunting deer. For a change he appeared sober, no jug of whiskey in sight. I spoke to him, and he nodded at me as I walked in. I went into our kitchen and poured myself a tall glass of lemonade with ice. With the entire afternoon stretched out in front of me, a leisurely day lounging in my bedroom with *The Three Musketeers* seemed like a relaxing way to wait until my mama got home.

I lay upon my bed and started reading my book. As I was wondering how Paris might have looked during the era depicted in the book, a drowsiness overtook me and I surrendered to my sleepiness.

When I woke later on the sun was disappearing from the sky. My room was bathed in the surreal light caused by twilight. Thirsty, I slurped at my room temperature lemonade, enjoying its sweetness mixed with bitterness. Lemonade is reminiscent of life.

I started towards my bedroom door, wondering idly what my mother would prepare for dinner. I opened the door and froze, paralyzed by the words I heard from downstairs.

"It's obvious to me you've resumed fucking your boy's father," Raymond said. My mind was whirling with confusion and curiosity, and I eased forward into the darkened hallway, straining to overhear the conversation.

"So? What business would it be of yours if I were? Is

that why you burned down the paper mill? As some form of revenge? Idiot. You and I haven't been intimate in any shape or fashion in at least five years," I heard my mother reply. "Matter of fact, I've had enough of this. When you made the agreement to marry me in exchange for money, you promised to be a father to my unborn child. You've never attempted to be a father to him. You sit here daily, brooding and silent. Living with you is like living with a breathing corpse. You eat and drink, but you don't live and you don't inspire life. In fact, when you walk your sorry ass out of here tonight, don't ever fucking come back! I'd rather spend the rest of my life as Bobby's mistress than to suffer another night with you under my roof. You hear that? My roof! With your sorry ass!" Her voice rose in volume with each word.

There was silence for a few seconds, my stomach was churning with the information I'd just learned, and I had new questions to add to my list. A life without Raymond's brooding presence would definitely be preferential to our current situation, and my heart smiled at the thought. And then the world shattered forever.

BOOM! BOOM!

I heard glass shattering and something slammed heavily into the living room wall. I was frozen, not believing what I'd just heard. I heard a sliding, metallic sound, then another BOOM shook the house. I heard what sounded like a bucket of water being thrown against the wall. Then it was silent again, and I hesitantly began walking downstairs. The smell of gunpowder was familiar to me, because I was from the country. Underneath the gunpowder smell was a heavy, rusty, metallic smell I wasn't familiar with. When I reached the bottom of the stairs and observed the wreckage of the living room, I knew what the metallic smell was. Blood.

I saw what remained of Raymond sitting on the couch, in the same spot I'd left him in many hours before. The shotgun he'd been polishing earlier was lying on the floor in front of him, resting at a crazy angle. I could see the stump of his spinal cord, the bloody bone sticking up where his head used to be. He'd blown his head completely off, his blood and brains splattered on the wall behind where his torso sat.

I looked at the opposite wall, noting the smashed glass everywhere. My beautiful mother lay at the base of the wall, her eyes open, staring at nothing. There were two saucer sized holes in her chest, pieces of her blouse visible in her wounds. Flora Jean was gone, and all my hopes and daydreams for us were gone as well. I sank to the floor, gathering my mother into my arms, and I wept uncontrollably. I cried for my mother, I sobbed for my grandmother, and I wept for myself.

No one came and I sat hugging my mother's lifeless body for hours. I made promises to my mother about the places I'd go and the things I'd see. Finally, I said goodbye to her and I stood up. My once pristine polo shirt was bloodstained, as were my bloody arms. I slowly walked through the glass on the floor to the telephone. As I lifted the receiver to call the police or ambulance, my eyes fixed on the clock hanging on the wall above Raymond's drying brain matter. The clock read 11:59, one minute before my thirteenth birthday.

# 4

# 11:59:11

As a daydreaming little boy in Mississippi, I dreamt of visiting the places I'd read about in books or saw in the movies. Right now though, I wish I was down in the Delta, sitting on my Grandma's porch, sipping a cold beer, and waving at the cars driving by. Life would be much simpler for me, if things and events had gone a different way. Maybe I'd be raising kids and fishing, waiting for the Friday night high school football game. As much as I'd hated Mississippi as a child, due to its racism and caste system, I think I'd have turned out all right if I'd stayed there. Nostalgic regrets, I guess.

"My mama is dead. They both are. Can you please

send help? I'm thirteen years old and I don't have anybody here with me," I said to the emergency dispatcher on the other end of the phone. She quickly assured me help was on the way. I hung up the phone and walked out onto the front porch to wait for the police to arrive. There was a slight breeze blowing, which on a typical night meant that the scents of the trees would have wafted in my direction. Maybe it did, but the smell of blood was too overpowering for me to smell anything else.

The first police car on the scene drove up to our house with the lights flashing, but no siren on. The paramedics pulled up right behind the police car. The dispatcher must have informed everyone there was no threat because both victims were already deceased. My appearance shocked them though, I could see it in their movements and expressions. The two cops looked at each other, then approached me with caution and suspicion apparent in their manner.

"What's going on? What happened?" the older officer asked. "Where are they?

I didn't say a word. I opened the front door and pointed. I knew I'd have to tell my story at some point, but I didn't want to keep having to repeat myself. Also, I hadn't made my mind up yet as to how much of the story I would keep to myself. There were still questions I needed answered, but there was only one person still living who could answer them—Bobby Fitzgerald Jr., my biological father.

As more cops and paramedics showed up on the scene, I idly wondered if there were any police officers anywhere else that night? We didn't live in a thriving metropolis which employed a whole bunch of cops. The drunks out driving home from the juke joints wouldn't have to worry about being pulled over because they were weaving or speeding, as every available police officer was at our house.

I was escorted upstairs to my bedroom by a relatively young police officer. He instructed me to put my shirt in an evidence bag, and to retrieve another. When I asked if I could wash my hands and arms, he shook his head and said no, because they'd need to run tests to see if I had gunshot residue on me. I looked perplexed and scared, but the police officer assured me the tests were policy, just to rule me out of the murder investigation.

After I changed shirts, the young police officer escorted me back down the stairs and then outside. There were at least ten cops there, along with paramedics and the now familiar face of the county coroner. I was placed in the back of a squad car, then driven to the police station, located in the town square.

Our town was probably a pretty good replica of every small southern town ever seen on television, or in the movies, or in old Norman Rockwell paintings. There was a town square, complete with a statue of a famous Mississippian, who happened to be a hero of the Confederacy. Multiple mom-and-pop stores surrounded the square, offering goods and services ranging from an ice cream parlor to a hardware store. In the middle of the square was the municipal building, which housed the town's government offices and the police station.

I was led in to the station, and the young police officer

who seemed to have been appointed my guide ran the residue tests before fingerprinting me. Afterwards, he led me to a washroom, where I vigorously washed my mother's blood off of me. The boy looking back at me from the mirror was not physically different from who I'd been the day before. The changes were all on the inside, and I could feel my emotions threatening to erupt. But who was left for me to be angry at? Only one name came to mind, and it was hard to be angry at Bobby Fitzgerald Jr., because I'd never personally interacted with the man. My eyes were red, and my face bore the tracks of my tears. I washed my face with cold water and exhaled. I would not have an emotional breakdown.

When I emerged from the washroom, I was a little surprised because the sheriff himself had come in for my interview. After I was seated across from the young police officer, Bobby Fitzgerald Jr. walked in. It was the first time I'd ever seen my biological father in the flesh. As he shook hands with the sheriff, I searched his face for similarities to my own which I'd just looked at in the washroom. Yeah, I saw the resemblances. Same eye shape, similarly colored eyes, his grayish-green, as were mine. We had the same forehead and aquiline nose, but my lips were fuller. If anyone knew our connection, they'd see the resemblance immediately. I wondered how big of a secret was my paternity.

Bobby Jr. strolled across the room, and sat himself down in the chair next to me. He didn't look at me, or pat me on the shoulder, he just sat there. I stopped staring at him, and I turned my attention to the young police officer sitting across from me.

He pushed the red button on the ancient tape recorder in front of him, and began the inquiry. I haltingly began to tell the story, my voice becoming stronger as the story unfolded from my mouth. The young police officer asked questions every few moments which I answered truthfully, for the most part.

Yes, I'd seen the shotgun before, but only if Raymond was going hunting. No, he'd never displayed violent tendencies towards my mother or myself. No, I can't say whether or not he was having a breakdown, because he and I didn't talk. The paper mill? No, I didn't hear anything about the fire.

By the time I got to the actual murder, Bobby Jr. looked pale and bothered. As if he were dreading my next words. I wanted to tell him not to worry, his name wouldn't come up. My mother had died in a terrible way, and out of respect for her I'd keep her secrets. Nobody else needed to know her business. A murder-suicide is scandalous in itself, no need to add even more scandal by mentioning my paternity.

"They started arguing as soon as she came in," I said. "I didn't hear exactly what set it off, but by the time I started heading for the living room, their voices got louder. She called him a bum and a loser, and then she told him to get out of our house and our lives forever. I heard the gunshots a few seconds later," I said.

It hurt to recall those painful moments again. A few tears rolled down my face, yet I continued to look steadily at the young police officer. The worst of my fears had already been realized, so I had nothing more to fear. I hoped they'd written down and recorded everything I said, because I knew I couldn't tell the story again for someone else. Not then at least.

The young police officer stopped the recorder. He stood, shook my hand, thanked me, and murmured his condolences. Then he, Bobby Jr., and the sheriff walked across the room to have a private conversation about me. Usually, in child welfare cases, a social worker would have been there on my behalf. Especially when me not having any family was factored in. I'm sure if it were a typical situation, I would have been placed under state care until a foster family was found. It was a grim situation which I'd been placed in, unable to control my own destiny.

What would become of me now? An orphaned boy, with no legally recognized relatives. Who would I be able to rely on for food, shelter, and comfort? Who would I have to turn to, on the nights when nightmares plagued my sleep? I had no one, and I thought of Oliver Twist, Johnny Tremain, and Edmond Dantes, literary heroes who had been alone in this world. Yet, somehow, they'd all survived. And even though their stories were fiction, I found hope in them.

The sheriff beckoned me over to where the three of them were standing. The young police officer patted me on the shoulder, then disappeared down a corridor. The sheriff looked me in the eye, but Bobby Jr. did not make eye contact. He looked away as if he would rather be anywhere else. So would I, I thought.

"Son, due to Mr. Fitzgerald being your mother's emergency contact and employer, we think it would be in your best interest to go home with him," the sheriff explained. "If we waited to see what Child Services might want to do, I don't think it would go so well for you. Mr. Fitzgerald has volunteered to make sure you're going to be all right, and I think that's best for all parties involved. What do you think?"

I thought about it, tilting my head downwards, as I stared down at my beat-up track shoes. If I didn't go with Bobby Jr., I might end up in a group home, or in the care of abusers. I looked up at the sheriff, and I slowly nodded my head. I didn't really have a choice.

A sheaf of papers was produced, which Bobby Jr. signed first. I was instructed to sign my name under his on each page, and the sheriff scrawled his signature under mine. They were release forms and acknowledgements for the most part. As I carefully signed my name on the first piece of paper, I thought to myself Bobby Jr.'s handwriting even resembled mine. Spooky.

I was led out of the police station by Bobby Jr., who still hadn't spoken directly to me. I followed him to his car, a late model Cadillac. After sitting down in the passenger seat, I understood the allure of Cadillacs. The seats were leather and there appeared to be polished wood-grain everywhere. The car was classy, yet comforttable. One day, I promised myself, I'd have a Cadillac of my own.

"I'll give you a brief overview of everything going on," he said, once the car started rolling. "I'm going to be your legal guardian from this point forward, until you are an adult. I will look out for your best interests until I feel you're mature enough to make your own decisions. That might happen way before you turn twenty-one, no one can predict stuff like that. I made a promise to Flora Jean I would always make sure you were all right. I'm sure you have questions about my relationship with your mother, but the past died with her, and it's no longer important. Right now, you and I need to concentrate solely on the future, understand?"

I nodded my head in assent, unsure then of his meaning but completely aware my life had changed drastically for better and for worse on my thirteenth birthday. As we rolled past the burned down shell of the paper mill, I wondered which domino would fall next.

# 5

# 11:59:12

A man without a moral compass will be lost all of his life, waxing and waning in an existence of indecisiveness. We may inherently know the difference between right and wrong, but we tend to make situational decisions based on whatever we're dealing with in that moment. What defines right or wrong? Simple. It depends on the situation we're facing.

The drive from the police station was utterly silent, not a word exchanged between us, nor was the radio on. Bobby Jr. pulled the Cadillac into the huge circular drive of the Fitzgerald estate, then he shut off the engine and began to talk.

"For the next few days you'll stay in the gatehouse where Jasper, our houseman, lives. He'll take care of all of your needs as far as food is concerned. I know you're a voracious reader, so I'll make sure you have all the books you'd like. Today I just need you to rest up, because the road ahead is looking pretty rocky. Any questions?"

"Why can't I stay in the main house? And when can I retrieve my things from my house?" I hadn't meant to ask the first question, but I couldn't help myself. Curiosity prodded the question out of me.

"You can't stay in the main house, because it would cause too many questions from my elderly mother, who knows nothing of your existence. My children have been shipped to their mother for the next week, freeing me up to deal with your situation," he said. "Tomorrow Jasper will drive you to your house, and he'll help you gather your important things. Afterward he'll take you shopping for clothes for school and the funeral. Next Sunday you'll be on a train heading north, because you'll be attending boarding school up there. I'm sorry, but I feel as if Mississippi is not a healthy place for your growth. You'll do better up there," he concluded. "Trust me."

Wow, Mr. Bobby Fitzgerald Jr. had mapped the next few years of my life out, and I had no say whatsoever in the matter. Such is the life of a pawn.

Jasper was an old Black man set in his ways, and aware of his place in the world. He didn't ask questions nor did he answer any. He guided me to a bedroom, and during the course of the day he brought me meals and made sure I was okay. Yet, he didn't say anything of importance to me.

The next day, after a sleepless night, I showered, then dressed myself in the same clothes I'd worn the day before. Jasper was standing in the kitchen, waiting for me. I glanced around the space, and on the refrigerator there was a small picture of a young woman. She was wearing a white sundress and smiling at the photographer. She was beautiful, and she looked as if she'd had the world on a string. It was a much younger version of my mother, Flora Jean.

"I've knowed your mama and Ms. Lily forever, it seems," the old man said. "It ain't easy to believe they both gone, and it's gonna be a long, hard road to healing. They was proud of you, and don't you forget that when you get out in the world. You represent they best hopes and wishes."

Jasper slid a plate of bacon, scrambled eggs, homemade biscuits, and fried green tomatoes in front of me. It was by no means an easy breakfast to prepare, and I nodded my thanks at him. He smiled at me, and placed a hand on my shoulder for a brief moment. I hadn't thought I had an appetite for breakfast, but I started eating, the food reminding me of how my grandma used to cook. I almost licked my plate clean, before remembering my manners. It was delicious, and I looked up at Jasper. His eyes were glistening as he watched me, and I realized I was not the only person in mourning.

A little while later we were in an older Cadillac, on our way to my house to gather my belongings. It was another one of those blisteringly hot days, and I was thankful for the air conditioning in the car. It was a surrealistic moment, crossing the threshold of my mama's house, going under and around the yellow tape denoting a murder scene. Jasper walked in with me, his hand on my shoulder, and I couldn't stop myself from looking at the wall where Raymond's brains had been splattered. The stain was still there, but the actual brain matter had mostly been removed, leaving a dull, rusty space on the wall. I didn't look at the spot where my mother's body had lain, being unsure if I could stand it. Instead I walked to the staircase and ascended to my bedroom, while Jasper stayed in the living room and smoked a cigarette.

I filled a suitcase with my most treasured possessions. I packed my books, a few articles of clothing, and a picture of my grandma, my mama, and me. One of the ladies at the church had taken the photo and we were at a church picnic, dressed in white and smiling from ear-to-ear. We looked happy in the picture, and it had only been taken a couple of years before. Things change fast. I wrapped the picture in between some t-shirts, then I wiped my tears and got on with what I was supposed to be doing.

I retrieved the money I'd been saving from a shoebox beneath my bed. I had close to six hundred dollars, which I hid inside of a pair of socks in my suitcase. Once the money was hidden, I closed the suitcase. Everything of value to me was now in one small suitcase. I took one last look around the room I'd slept in all of my life. I'd daydreamed of many things in my bedroom, and I wondered when or if I would ever have a home again. I then went back downstairs and out of the door, looking neither to my right or left, doing my best to erase the images of blood and brains from my memory. Jasper exited the house before me, and I closed the door with a finality, leaving my childhood home behind.

In the following days leading up to my mother's funeral I finished *The Three Musketeers*, returned it to the library, and I didn't read Dumas for at least another ten years. Jasper kept me well-fed and he helped to shop for clothes, luggage, and school supplies. I didn't see Bobby Jr. at all during the entire week. I always called him Bobby Jr. in my head because any other title wouldn't feel right. Dad? Never. My father? Only through DNA.

The church was filled to capacity when Jasper and I arrived, adding to my sense of déjà vu. It took the lack of lilies everywhere to convince me I wasn't reliving the same nightmare of my grandma's funeral. Jasper walked to the front row with me and I sat down, facing my mother's casket. I couldn't go and look at her lying in the casket, for fear I might lose it and start screaming. I sat in that by myself, accepting hugs, kisses, and handshakes as the mourners filed past my mother's casket. The organist was playing doleful music until finally, the ushers closed her casket, and the preacher began the eulogy.

To this day, I couldn't tell you any of the subjects the reverend preached about. My mind was dwelling on early morning walks with Flora Jean, trips to the library, ice cream cones, my mama's easy laughter, her constant singing, and a million other memories which I would never experience again. A steady stream of tears rolled down my face, and when the choir began to sing *His Eye is on the Sparrow*, whimpering sounds escaped from my soul. No one heard them, because no one was next to me. I had no one anymore. I was alone in this world.

After the reading of Flora Jean's obituary the reverend had the ushers reopen the casket. Once again, the mourners trudged by it. After the last person had walked by the reverend looked at me imploringly, as if to remind me this would be the last time I would ever see my mama's face, until we met again in Eternity. I steeled myself, then rose and slowly walked the twelve feet to her casket, and I looked upon her face. I leaned over and kissed her, my tears dripping onto her face. I whispered to her, "Goodbye Mama," before the ushers closed her casket for the last time.

As I walked back toward the pew my burning eyes scanned the church. He was standing in an alcove towards the back of the church. His eyes met mine, and I nodded my head in Bobby Jr.'s direction. At least he came. Jasper led me out of the church, and he and I rode in silence to the cemetery.

The mourners gathered around the grave, and I sat in a chair four feet from the hole in the ground. The choir sang a final song, *Going up Yonder* softly, as if they didn't want to wake Flora Jean. As their final notes died away, it seemed as if the birds had stopped twittering. Silence reigned, as if the entire universe had stopped for a moment. I felt a hand on my shoulder, causing me to look up hopefully and expectantly. Nope, it was only Jasper, offering me comfort as best he could. I still wonder why Bobby Jr. had not been the one to comfort me, or at least sit next to me. Maybe he'd been too consumed with his own grieving. He hadn't shown up to the cemetery.

The reverend delivered a final prayer for my mama, and a church member handed me a lily to toss onto the casket as it began to descend into the ground. It was over and the mourners began to disperse, some offering words of comfort, others just melting away. There would be no repast for Flora Jean, even though her church had volunteered. I'd declined to attend, remembering how she'd danced and laughed not too long before at my grandma's.

Finally, it was only Jasper and me remaining at the gravesite. I tossed a red rose down into the grave and when it landed on the casket, something amazing happened. The air around me was suddenly filled with fluttering butterflies in every shade of the rainbow. I hadn't seen them during the service, and their sudden flight made it seem as if they had been attending Flora Jean's burial, and knew it was over. I watched the butterflies soar, and then disappear into the blue sky.

The gravediggers had waited respectfully a few feet away, letting me have the final moments with my mother. The butterflies leaving was my signal it was time for me to go. I was ready now, ready to move on from this place and these memories.

"Let's go," I said to Jasper. I rose from my chair and nodded to the gravediggers, letting them know they could fill in her grave. I started walking to the car, when Jasper gently grabbed me by my arm.

"Not yet," he said. "We have another stop to make first."

He guided me deeper into the cemetery, towards the rear. I was puzzled by this, but I was too tired to question him. He must've had his reason, but to this day I still can't figure it out.

Gathered around an open grave were three men, passing around a bottle of whiskey between them. These men were vaguely familiar to me, but my tired mind couldn't place them. One of them took the bottle of whiskey and poured some into the open grave. He looked into my puzzled eyes and began to speak.

"It didn't make sense to rent a hall because no one would show up, and it was doubtful if anyone would've rented a hall to us. Same with the churches. So here we are, Raymond's friends, to say goodbye to him," the man said.

My mouth dropped in horror, and I turned a furious look toward Jasper. This was the final goodbye for the man who had murdered my mother, butchered my childhood, and destroyed all I had ever known. Before I could make my outburst, Jasper spoke first.

"You can hate him, but you can't judge him, because you will never know what demons drove him and destroyed him. One day, your hate may change to pity. I pray for your sake, you'll find pity in your heart for Raymond."

I quietly took in his words, and the three men began to fill in Raymond's grave. As Jasper and I walked to the car, I contemplated Jasper's words. Yes, Raymond had murdered my mother, then himself, because he had lost all hope for happiness, or so I thought.

Now, looking back on the whole situation, I'm appreciative to Jasper for taking me to Raymond's burial. Five people were at his burial, no reverend, no choir, no flowers, and no tears. A murderer's funeral, acknowledged with a pint of whiskey, shared by his three cronies. Murderers don't even deserve that much, or do they?

# 6

## 11:59:15

When a person has witnessed the worst aspects of human behavior, nothing else will ever shock them again. In fact, some of the most heinous and vile acts won't even be considered shocking anymore. When one's psyche becomes conditioned to always expect the worst, the only surprises come when something good occurs. Because we never expect good things to happen anymore.

The morning after my mother's funeral, Jasper drove me and all of my possessions to the train depot. Bobby Jr. hadn't even taken the time to say goodbye or wish me well. I should have known. Jasper helped me get situated, then he shook my hand and said goodbye. I never saw him again. As he walked away, I realized that Jasper had been the only male adult in my life to treat me with any sort of concern. I watched him go and wondered to myself about his relationships with my mother and grandma. I should have asked more questions.

Indiana. I was being sent "Up North" to the Boniface School for Boys. Bobby Jr. had made sure to leave an information packet with Jasper for me to take with me. Of course I opened it, planning to read it to pass the time. Copies of my birth certificate and my school records were enclosed. On my birth certificate Raymond was listed as the father, even though he wasn't.

I'd dreamt of leaving Mississippi for so long, but the reality was daunting. As the train chugged past cornfields and sleepy little towns, I didn't know what was going to happen next. I'd only read about boarding schools, or I'd seen grim depictions of them in movies. I vowed to myself I wouldn't cry publicly, nor would I let anyone make me think less of myself. I was determined to be as adult-like as I could, because there was no one left who would treat me like a child. I grew up during my train ride, or at least I did mentally. No matter what was in store for me at Boniface, how bad could it be? Ha, I vastly underestimated the experience I was to endure over the next few years.

Bobby Jr. had decided Mississippi wasn't healthy for me. No discussion with me or anything. In hindsight, I should have spoken up. I should have fought for more of a say in my life. No matter what scandals and secrets would have surrounded me, I had already proven I wasn't weak. I was thirteen years old, and the only friends I'd ever had were my mama and grandma. Maybe I could have gone to school in Mississippi with Jasper as my caretaker. Maybe he'd have been the mentor I needed. Maybe he'd have taken the paternal role which I lacked. He might even have taken me fishing. Maybe things in my life would have turned out differently if I'd used my voice to speak up.

The Boniface School was located twenty-five miles west of South Bend, Indiana. Chicago was only an hour or so away, but as it were, I was surrounded by cornfields, Amish settlements, and people who lacked melanin. I found out the harshness of being the only so-called Black person in a lily-white environment.

A car from the school was waiting for me when I stepped out of the train station. It was a stately, black sedan, and it transported me to my new home, where I'd spend the majority of the next few years of my life. When I got out of the car, I stood there on the sidewalk with my luggage. I looked around at my new surroundings. Boniface had multiple buildings, large and small, a gymnasium, a greenhouse, dormitories, and of course, a building for staff and classrooms. I'd learn there were only 350 students, ranging in age from thirteen to eighteen. From Boniface, graduating students matriculated to either college or the military. For it to be a Midwestern school, it had a fine and storied pedigree. Senators, scholars, scientists, and generals had graduated from Boniface. As had Bobby Jr., which was why he must have felt it would be a good experience for me, as it must have been for him.

11:59

As I struggled through the main door with my luggage, the dean of the school awaited me. He helped me with my belongings, then we walked toward his office. As we walked he introduced himself as Dean Jarrett, pointing out the directions to the library, classrooms, and lunchroom, where I'd eat three meals a day. Upon entering his richly furnished office, we left my luggage by the entrance, and Dean Jarrett bade me to sit down.

"As a new student here at Boniface, I will go over a few things with you, in order to make sure your time here is beneficial," Dean Jarrett said. "Normally, at most schools, your syllabus and grade level are determined by your age. We do things quite differently here. Tomorrow morning you'll spend your first academic day taking placement tests. Then we'll construct your schedule based on your test scores. Extracurricular activities are strongly encouraged, and I believe we have something for everyone. With all of that being said, welcome to Boniface, and I hope you'll do well here."

He then shook my hand, and gave me directions to my dorm room. I gathered my things and I followed his directions to my dorm room, my new home. When entering into a new world, it's usually best to have a clear knowledge of one's self. I really had no clue at the time about who I was as a person. I couldn't call myself friendly, because I had yet to experience friendship with a peer. I'd never been put to the test of keeping someone else's secrets, because no one had ever shared a secret with me. I felt as if the open secret of my paternity wasn't really something which had been shared with me, so it didn't count. As I entered my dorm room, my hope was to one day have a friend and confidante with whom to share hopes, dreams, and secrets.

My roommate turned out to be a small, pudgy, bespectacled boy from Chicago named Jerry Goldstein. He shook my hand upon my entrance, and helped me to get settled on my side of our room. As I unpacked my things, Jerry gave me a better overview of life at Boniface than Dean Jarrett had. Jerry broke down the caste system to me. The moneyed students from rich families were at the top of the pyramid, setting the school trends because they were the most popular and emulated. The middle tier, according to Jerry, was made up of the athletes. The bottom tier consisted of scholarship kids, of which Jerry was one, and the minorities. He was basically letting me know where I stood in the hierarchy at Boniface.

I took placement tests in a variety of core subjects the next morning. My results were in by lunchtime, and had been impressive enough for me to be placed in freshman classes, even though I hadn't graduated from grade school. My happiness over my results didn't last very long, because the reality of Boniface wiped any traces of happiness away. By the end of my first week there, so many realizations had become abundantly clear to me.

At least at home in Mississippi there'd been other people who looked like me. Even though my former classmates had not embraced me as a friend, they had not gone out of their way to make my life miserable. I was the lone Black student at the school, which made blending in an impossibility. At least in Mississippi, I'd have had the familiarity of home to help buffer my isolation. At first, the sly and muttered remarks went over my head.

When I realized the butt of their jokes was me, I knew what was in store for the rest of my time at Boniface. No matter what had been said to me back home, I wasn't prepared for the viciousness.

As the only Black in an all-white world, I always felt like the target. I tried my best to ignore all of it, but even my best efforts couldn't prevent the slurs from getting under my skin. Maybe I'd have weathered the storm better if I'd had someone to talk to. Jerry was a good roommate, but we didn't ever become friends, because I was wary of him as well. He never joined in with any of the others, as far as ostracizing me, but he didn't take up for me either. When we were in our room we were cordial, but he'd be on his computer, and I'd be reading one of my books.

If one of my teachers made a reference to Africa, slaves, Dr. King, or animals, the whispered jokes and giggles would start. The teachers would only attempt to hush the noise if they got too loud. In the beginning of my first semester there it was more subtle, but by October it was non-stop and aggressive.

"There's fried chicken being served for dinner, better get there before the Midnight Marauder."

"These biscuits remind me of someone's lips."

"Probably the first one in his family to walk upright."

I knew if I had a physical confrontation with any of them I'd probably be expelled, or they'd jump me. The treatment I received pushed me even deeper into myself. I nursed my hurts and licked my wounds, managing to keep my fists and words to myself. Thus I learned how to hate. I was still too much of a wounded juvenile to realize people will always find a reason to mock, taunt, or dislike another person. All they need is someone to point them in the right direction as to where to focus their disdain. Followers only need a leader. It didn't take me too long to realize the leader and most outspoken of my tormentors was a boy named Lars Nicholls Jr.

# 7

# 11:59:16

In my life, the intensity of my emotions has gotten the best of me on a lot of occasions. Anxiety, anger, hate, and love. Most of my actions or reactions were caused by those feelings. Less intense emotions such as empathy or apathy didn't move me at all. I didn't feel much sympathy, because I always selfishly felt as if no one had a worse time of it than me. As far as apathy, if I had no feelings towards you, then you didn't count on my emotional barometer. Bobby Jr. mostly fell into the apathetic category as my life went on.

In November of my first year at Boniface I made the decision to join the chess team. I probably could have attempted to ingratiate myself by joining the basketball or football teams, but I felt it would have been expected of the lone Black student. Nope. In chess, it's always one-on-one, and the team only wins if the majority of the matches were conquered by either school. Chess was an individual sport, where fake high fives and chest bumps weren't requirements.

Chess spoke to my cunning, analytical side. It had always been intriguing to me, causing me to read up on it and learn the rules and the moves. By the time I joined the team I was a chess addict. I'd read the history of chess, learning it was originally created to teach military strategy. The game of chess encouraged me to start using chess strategies in life, viewing every situation as if it were a chessboard, and my move was next. Chess lessons came in handy when dealing with adversity, such as my racist, elitist classmates.

For every slight and insult hurled at me, I would devise a response based on chess, as to the appropriate countermove. I didn't act on most of my thoughts, but sometimes just the process of thinking out a plan of retribution was enough to clear my mind from pursuing revenge. Impulsive people make hasty, irrational decisions, and I was determined to not be a slave to my emotions.

I wasn't a child anymore, not really. I was an orphan who needed to look out for myself as much as possible. In the spirit of trying to appear more mature, I put aside the name "Robby." It had been my mother's name for me, and I buried the name in my memory. Sure, I could have let the other students and faculty address me as Robert, or maybe even Rob. A couple of times other students attempted to address me as Bobby. I shut all of that down, insisting on being addressed as Jackson. Yes, it was the name of a murderer, but there were dozens of boys named Robert or Bobby at Boniface. There was only one Jackson. I'm not going to relive and retell every single event which happened in my time at Boniface. I'll touch on the poignant events which helped or guided me to becoming my present self. The past always shapes the future, no matter how much we pretend it doesn't.

Having joined the chess team my next hurdle was the approaching holidays of Thanksgiving and Christmas. Holidays are important, cherished because of the memories we accumulate over our lifetimes. For some, it might be memories of snowball fights or particular Christmas gifts which became treasured belongings. Until then, my Thanksgiving had consisted of my grandma's stuffed turkey, roasted ham, and other traditional foods. Christmas had been the opening of presents with my mama, laughter, and the feeling of joy. Now, I'd have to find some new meaning of my own in the holiday season.

I received a message from Dean Jarrett's office to return a phone call from Bobby Jr. I called as soon as I had time, from the office of the dean. Bobby Jr.'s secretary, Ms. Lenora, put my call through to him, and we had what I like to think of as my "Eureka" conversation. Bobby Jr. inquired as to how I was doing educationally, even though I'm sure he stayed abreast of my grades. I responded to all of his questions with the same words, over and over.

"Everything is fine," I lied. The truth wouldn't change anything. The treatment from my schoolmates, he couldn't do anything about it. Unless it was to transfer me to another school, where the ostracizing process might possibly recur or be even worse. He couldn't bring my mother or grandmother back from beyond to help with my feelings of loneliness and abandonment. Therefore, I kept it all to myself, which became a habitual thing for me. Everything is fine.

He inquired as to whether or not I'd like to come to Mississippi during the holidays, where I could stay with Jasper, dine with Jasper, and celebrate the holidays with Jasper. The guy never mentioned spending any time with him or his two other children, which meant I was and would always be a secret. I pretended to be fine with that. I asked what my alternatives were, explaining to him my reluctance to return to Mississippi.

"There's nothing there for me," I said. "Spending the holidays with Jasper is not my idea of a homecoming, and bad memories and experiences would be the only things I could be sure about. What are my other alternatives?"

"If you would like, my secretary can arrange for your vacations, and will take care of your travel expenses and lodging," he said. "I just need you to make your requests or desires known at least a month ahead of time. For Thanksgiving week, Christmas break, spring vacation, and summer vacation, you'll need to research any trips you'd like to make. There'll be some places I'll insist you go, but I think you'll like my decisions."

Since I really had no idea as to what I'd like to do for Thanksgiving, I acquiesced to whatever he thought was best, as long as it wasn't Mississippi. In Mississippi I was his dirty little secret, his love child, and publicly known as the boy whose parents had been involved in a horrible murder/suicide. I didn't want any part of it. Hiding out in the gatehouse, unworthy and unwanted in the main house. Jasper was a nice old guy, but there was nothing in Mississippi for me.

For Thanksgiving I spent the week at a bed and breakfast in the area, fortified with my books and my chessboard. It was in southwestern Michigan, and I spent my days walking different beaches, and being amazed at the various lighthouses which abounded in the area. I tried to imagine the lonely existence the lighthouse keepers had endured, and I realized their existence wasn't too far removed from my own.

I actually enjoyed my solitude while I was there. I walked, practiced chess moves, and I did a lot of reading. I had a problem with so-called "classic" novels because nothing about them appealed to me, making me wonder who had deemed these books classics? I kept attempting to read the tale of the great whale, and it kept putting me to sleep. I wondered if it was due to the walking, or the three sumptuous meals a day I was consuming, but as the same result happened on the short train ride back to school, I knew it was the book. I left it on the train.

When I returned to Boniface I began researching new and different destinations, so I'd have my plans ready for every vacation going forward. As long as I knew where I wanted to go, everything would be fine, or at least that's what I assumed.

I hadn't counted on Bobby Jr. insisting every trip I

desired to take must have some educational merit. That ruled out Disney World or any place similar to it. I'd figure out eventually how to incorporate roller-coasters and theme parks into my trips. It was another lesson on the need to incorporate the moves of chess into my life. In order to achieve the things I wanted to in life, I'd have to always stay a few moves ahead of Bobby Jr. and anyone else.

Between playing chess, staying ahead of my peers in my studies, and planning my vacations, I was able to ignore the bullshit I dealt with daily. I figured four years would go faster as long as I used my vacations and eventual escape as dangling carrots to keep me motivated. I knew I would persevere, simply because I had no other choice.

The rest of my first year at Boniface went better than I'd had any right to expect. For Christmas, I spent three weeks in Chicago, familiarizing myself with the layout and the culture of the city. Bobby Jr.'s secretary, Ms. Lenora, was my communication conduit to my father. She made my hotel reservations, travel accommodations, and she helped me set up a bank account, naming herself as the administrator. Deposits would be made by her prior to every trip. I had a bank card, which allowed me to withdraw money as I needed. On a whim, I had Ms. Lenora set up a personal savings account, which gave me somewhere to deposit the cash I'd brought from Mississippi, $600. Not too shabby for a thirteen-year-old orphan.

Chicago during the Christmas season was amazing, with parades, ice skating, carolers, decorations everywhere, and a holiday spirit which helped to somewhat combat my loneliness and mourning. My hotel was located downtown, and I only had to sign for meals. On Christmas morning I received an extra $500 in my account, accompanied by a telegram from Bobby Jr. telling me to buy myself something nice. I'm pretty sure Ms. Lenora was responsible for the unexpected bonus, because the gift was too thoughtful and kind, unlike my normal interactions with him.

Banking and finance were intriguing to me, and after the Christmas break I began to learn the nuances of banking and money management. I knew one day I wouldn't want Bobby Jr. in charge of my finances, because one's power over money equates to control over someone's life. I wouldn't be under his thumb any longer than necessary.

I was diligent in my studies, maintaining straight As in all of my subjects. I loved books, so being the best student wasn't an issue for me. Yet I never raised my hand in class to answer a question, nor did I go out of my way to shine the spotlight on myself. My instructors knew the type of student I was, yet they didn't thrust me into the spotlight, probably because they knew I didn't crave the attention. I didn't need anything extra to draw the ire of my contemporaries.

For spring break I journeyed back to Chicago for a week, still a bit hesitant to spread my wings. I visited the various world-renowned museums, devoured the Chicago-style food, and I went to a baseball game, just to experience it. The baseball game experience taught me to never again attend an April baseball game there, because it was a bone-chilling event. I learned it is best to wait until late May or June before going to a game, because the weather is more predictable then. I started preparing myself for my next trip, mentally ready for more new experiences. One other lesson I learned from my Chicago trip was how no one really pays much attention to a kid alone. Especially if the child is well-mannered and decently attired. As long as I didn't draw attention to myself, I could move through the world almost invisibly.

After spring break, as the school year wound down, I received a phone call from Ms. Lenora, informing me of the plans Bobby Jr. had made for my summer vacation. I was going to a camp for chess players in Ohio, maybe one hundred miles east of South Bend. I would eat three times a day, discuss chess, and learn more tricks and traps than I already knew. So, basically, even though he never communicated with me personally, he was well aware of my activities and my skills. I'd bear that in mind for future reference.

# 8

## 11:59:19

Environment is the most dominant factor in the overall makeup of a typical human being. A child who grows up poor, but beloved by its family, will probably grow up to be a productive member of society, one who'll place family before money. We're familiar with these types, the ones who'll eschew promotions and money in order to spend more time with their families. We cynics regard these types as simpletons, yet underneath our cynicism lies a small bit of envy.

Then there are those who grew up poor and unloved. Typically, the value of money far outweighs the value of family or friendship. Money is the antidote for the formerly unloved, used as a balm for the unhealed scars carried within. As time moved on I realized without a doubt I was different, fitting into neither category. Money was important to me, because maybe it was the key needed to create my own familial bonds.

I spent the first summer as an orphan at a chess camp not too far from Sandusky, Ohio. The camp was helpful as far as chess was concerned. The other campers were cordial enough, but something in me just wouldn't allow me to put myself out there in order to become friends with someone. Maybe someone should write a book titled *Making Friends for Dummies*. I'm sure it would be a bestseller. If my idea sparks someone to decide to write it, I hope they cut me in, or at least mention my name.

The other bonus from the first summer was the location of the camp, just outside of Sandusky. There's an amusement park located in Sandusky which is billed as the "Rollercoaster Capital of the World." Yes, I went to the amusement park and rode roller-coasters for the first time in my life. It was an enjoyable, slightly bittersweet moment, because Flora Jean should have been with me. As I had gone down my first dip on the first coaster, I closed my eyes in remembrance of my mama, because she'd have loved it.

When I returned for school in August I was fourteen years old, and I'd grown five inches. I informed Ms. Lenora of my growth spurt, and she promptly made arrangements by sending me new uniforms, new jackets, shoes, and what she referred to as "play clothes," jeans and t-shirts. I was grateful for her, and I wondered if she took care of all of Bobby Jr.'s business or just the things he couldn't be bothered with, like me.

I was a little disheartened to find upon my return my roommate Jerry had left school. I received an enthusiastic letter from him, saying he'd been accepted into one of the more prestigious high schools in Chicago, and even better, it was free. He inquired as to how I was doing, and encouraged me to be strong amidst the rancor of my schoolmates. Looking back now, I realize Jerry could have been a friend if only I'd have let him. He'd been in a similar situation while at Boniface, due to him being bookish as well as Jewish. I responded to his letter, but I was nowhere near as forthcoming about my thoughts as he had been in his letter. I mailed it off, and instantly regretted it. My response seemed more like a business communication than a personal letter, and suffice it to say, we didn't keep up our correspondence. I regret it now, because it could have been a major turning point in my life to have a friend. I missed out twice on a friendship opportunity with Jerry.

I was now five-foot-ten, and my new height seemed to quiet down a lot of the malicious remarks from my schoolmates. They murmured to each other but if I glared at them, they'd shut up, looking elsewhere, as if they hadn't been talking about me.

I realized, as the year went on, the cowardice of almost all of them. They wouldn't even look me in the eyes if they were alone. Yet, if it were a group of them, they were emboldened by the presence of their compatriots. I learned to avoid groups of them, but I'd cower them with a look if they were alone. They were a bunch of cowardly followers, influenced by the actions and words of one boy, their leader, Lars Nicholls Jr.

Lars Nicholls Jr. was a blond, blue-eyed god at Boniface. Everyone looked up to him as their leader because he was the varsity quarterback, and hailed from one of the richest families in the Midwest. Some boys are built for the mantle of leadership and admiration, but Lars was not made to be an empathetic leader. If he had been king of a small nation, the people would have cheered him publicly, while privately hoping for an assassination. It wasn't in him to be kind or caring, because he looked down upon everyone with an ingrained and malicious sense of superiority. He was my worst antagonist and the ringleader behind all of the shitty racism I faced.

One morning I fixed my plate in the cafeteria, but I had neglected to grab silverware. I set my tray down at an unoccupied table. I had to go back to the beginning of the line in order to pick up a knife, fork, and spoon. As I walked back towards the table where I'd left my tray of food, I watched horrified as Lars hawked up a loogie and spit his mucus into my breakfast. I stopped in my tracks, gripping the butter knife as if it were a dagger. I was ready to attack him, to stab, bite, beat, and pummel, but even more, I wanted to scream my hatred of Lars and his pals to the world. Instead, I remained silent and did nothing, while he and his followers laughed in my face. I did not eat breakfast that morning.

My revenge fantasies no longer included the sidekicks, the followers, or the hangers on. No, they centered around Lars, visions of him bloody and on his knees begging for mercy. The thirst for some form of revenge flitted in and out of my mind constantly. I was confident I could beat him in a fistfight, but the repercussions might have been disastrous. I may have been expelled from Boniface and recalled to Mississippi by Bobby Jr., and forced to finish my schooling there. I ruled out a physical confrontation, knowing there must be another route to revenge. I thought about all sorts of schemes and plans, but none of my ideas seemed possible or plausible to me, at least not then.

Jerry was never replaced by another student, and I had my room to myself for the remaining years at Boniface. Having the entire room allowed me to spread out my belongings, which was a plus. I had my schoolbooks, posters of faraway places, and a table where my chessboard was always set up for practice. The flipside of not having a roommate was I didn't talk to anyone my age, because I did not converse with any of the other students.

I returned to Chicago for Thanksgiving, explored Indianapolis for Christmas, and enjoyed a bed and breakfast alongside Lake Michigan's eastern shore for spring break. I didn't venture too far away from Boniface for my vacations, but my world was growing in leaps and bounds in another way. Besides chess and finance, I found another interest to take hold of my brain; I discovered foreign languages.

Second-year students were required to take a foreign language, so I'd taken Spanish. Over the course of the year I discovered many of the European languages sprang from the same root language, Latin. I mastered Spanish over the course of the year, and when Bobby Jr. decreed I was to spend my summer on a cattle ranch in Nebraska, I bought books on beginning Latin, French, Italian, and

Portuguese. I figured I'd have plenty of time over the summer to learn the basics. I knew it would be smart to start with the Latin, because even though it was a dead language, it held the key to all of the other ones.

My second summer flew by, and not only did I learn the rudiments of those languages, I learned to ride and saddle a horse, throw a lasso, and shoot a gun. Rifles and pistols were easy enough to learn at the ranch, just part of the everyday lessons the ranch owner taught to the ten teenagers whose families had paid for them to be there. Ranching toughens a person up, mentally and physically, between rising well before the sun, wrestling with cattle, and becoming the caretaker for my assigned horse. I wouldn't mind owning a horse one day, but I'd have to own enough space. Horses needed room, meaning I'd need to own plenty of acreage.

Not only was I continuing to grow in stature, but I began to fill out more, no longer just tall, but thicker in my arms and legs as well. I caught myself looking in the mirror and being amazed and proud of how I looked. I could possibly be mistaken for a full-grown man. I was even beginning to sprout a few hairs on my chin. I didn't quite understand why I'd been sent to Nebraska, but I started to think Bobby Jr. had a plan for my future he hadn't informed me of yet. He was adding too many things to my toolbox, too many skills I couldn't understand the need for. I had the feeling he, too, was playing chess.

As a third-year student I remained a willing loner, no longer verbally assaulted to my face, but ostracized in other ways just the same. It didn't matter to me, as I was counting the days until my imprisonment at Boniface was over. I believe even if a student had made friendly overtures or gestures toward me, I would have rebuked their advances, not trusting them at all. I continued to excel in my studies, with my chess playing reaching new heights, and my planned vacations becoming a lot more daring.

For Thanksgiving that year I went to Boston, exploring the region where Thanksgiving and the Revolutionary War had been hatched. I met the ocean for the first time, and not even pictures of it had really expressed its vast beauty. It was a clear, chilly day, and the ocean and the sky were the same shades of blue, extending east as far as the eye could see. I felt small as I stood there, and I imagined the Pacific would be more of the same. I put it on my list of places to visit.

For Christmas I spent the break in New York City, exploring the boroughs, museums, delicatessens, and notable places, while riding and learning the subway system during the daytime. I stayed pretty close to my Midtown hotel at night, as I'd promised Ms. Lenora I would. I was able to witness the New Year's celebration in Times Square, and the times I'd seen it on television had not prepared me for the revelry I experienced in person. As the apple dropped and reached the end of its journey, signaling the New Year, an attractive, drunken woman kissed me fully on the mouth, probably not caring or realizing she was the first woman I'd ever kissed on the lips. I spent the rest of the night in my hotel room, daydreaming about kissing, touching, and exploring the fascinating world of women. Yes, I was becoming more worldly, but I was a teenaged boy dealing with raging hormones and lusty imaginings.

I turned sixteen the summer after my third year at Boniface, and I was no longer as unsure about the myriad of dilemmas which had once plagued my mind. I was the focus of my own intentions, and I would be the person who brought my dreams to fruition, regardless of the plans and machinations of Bobby Jr.

I spent that summer in Chicago, interning as an office boy at the Mercantile Exchange. I was steadfast in my efforts, constantly learning, always observing, and I constantly planned. I seriously thought of going to college in Chicago, but I wasn't quite ready to make my choice. I wanted to visit a couple of other cities and areas before making my choice.

I learned to drive a car that summer, receiving my license the day I turned sixteen. Freedom was getting closer, close enough for me to taste. I also ordered my passport, after learning I could get it on my own. My plans were becoming more concrete,  and my thoughts were more cosmopolitan regarding my outlook on life. I was a cynic, expecting the worst of everyone, in order never to be surprised again. Yet there was an underlying hope within my soul that I was on the cusp of finding some sort of happiness, some new kind of relationship. I already knew not to put too much stock in anyone.

Entering the school year, I knew what I wanted to accomplish during my final year at Boniface. I wanted to find the college of my choice, I wanted to be the valedictorian of my graduating class, I wanted to inflict revenge upon Lars Nicholls Jr. for the treatment I'd received at Boniface, and I needed to find out how it felt to make love to a woman. If I could accomplish the items on my checklist, the future would definitely be brighter than the past.

# 9

# 11:59:21

In the life of a male child, I feel as if certain rites of passage require the attention and guidance of a male parent. If there is no father available, then an uncle or grandfather or older brother should be present in teaching a young man the ropes and guidelines on the road to manhood. Little League baseball, how to ride a bike, change a tire, drive a car, shave, throw a football, and how to make romantic connections with the fairer sex. Mothers do the best they can when required to play both parental roles, but the absence of a father figure leaves a huge void in the development of a man, at least in my opinion.

Due to my mother's early departure into Eternity, and Bobby Jr.'s omnipotent, omniscient, yet absent approach to my development, I relied on books to teach me how to do most things. I didn't have friends to compare notes with, so I was on my own. I'd learned to drive, speak multiple languages, and most of my other mental skills from books. Yet books were sadly deficient in teaching me about the nuances of courtship, love, and women in a practical sense. The characters in the books I loved did not have sure-fire methods of attracting and keeping the attention of a woman, and their courtships were often accidental happenings. I wanted to be ahead of the game when it came to dating, which shows my naiveté.

When I experienced my first nocturnal emission, I thought I was having some kind of anxiety attack. While asleep, I'd dreamt of making love to a beautiful woman, whose face wasn't clear to me, but her body was. Ripe and lush in all places, I'd been kissing and fondling this faceless woman, when some kind of spasm overtook me. I awoke sweating, still shaking, my underwear wet and sticky, my penis throbbing and hard. Disgusted and scared, I hurried to the washroom to clean myself off, seriously considering calling the school nurse. I returned to my room and threw that underwear into the garbage. I opened up my computer, and waited while this new thing called the World Wide Web, or Internet, booted itself up. I typed in my symptoms and learned I wasn't in danger of dying, I'd only had a wet dream. See what I mean about a boy needing guidance from a male mentor?

Over the next couple of months, I experienced recurring wet dreams. My research led me to believe the way to slow them down was to actually have sex, alone or with someone else. I tried the alone angle a few times, but it left me feeling nasty and slimy, ashamed about my actions. I abandoned masturbation early on and turned my focus to how I could have sex with an actual woman.

There was an all-girls school not far from Boniface, but we only interacted with those girls at sports events and holiday mixers, neither of which I ever attended. My wet underwear and aching wrist led me to the conclusion I needed to change my thoughts about the nearby debutantes. I attended the football games, hoping to make a connection, but the only girl I found myself attracted to already had a boyfriend, the star quarterback at Boniface. Yeah, her boyfriend was Lars Nicholls Jr. It lessened my opinion of the young lady, because I couldn't understand how she could not see him for the jerk he was, not yet realizing people only see what they want to see in another person.

I attempted conversations with some of the other girls, trying to make any sort of connection, but my attempts fizzled out early on in those exchanges. I'd watch the girls walk away from me, then they'd giggle with their friends about my lame approach. Maybe I just wasn't their type, or maybe it was something else about me which frightened them. Or maybe I wasn't confident enough to bullshit my way into their hearts and underwear. There was a lot I needed to learn.

I stood in the corner, dejected, as I watched another young lady scurry away from me. I had attended the annual Halloween mixer in order to meet a girl, any girl, but my efforts were fruitless. As I sipped a bitter punch, a trio of older women walked past me. The one in the front was a short redhead, lushly built, with the undefinable air of someone who's comfortable in their own skin, regardless of where they might be. My breath caught just a little, and my heart almost stopped when the delectable redhead was addressed as "Mrs. Nicholls."

I was stunned to discover this amazing creature was the mother of my nemesis and most loathsome detractor, Lars Nicholls Jr. I stole quite a few looks at Mrs. Nicholls over the course of the evening, and by the end of the party my chess instincts had kicked in. It was time to make an opening move.

As the students exited the party Mrs. Nicholls and several other ladies shook the hands of departing students, even exchanging pleasantries with a few. I waited for my opportunity and when Mrs. Nicholls became available, I stepped in front of her and politely stuck out my hand.

"Hello ma'am, thank you for a wonderful party tonight," I said. She looked at me politely, and shook my hand gently. As she attempted to withdraw her hand, I held onto it for a couple of extra seconds. "My name is Jackson, and I'm looking forward to the next fundraising event, Mrs. Nicholls," I said, smiling as I released her hand.

She smiled at me. "Thank you, Jackson, and I'll see you next time," she said.

I exited the party, filled with purpose, feeling sure of a plan which I had hatched when I saw Lars Nicholls' mother. Pawn two spaces forward. *Let the games begin*, I thought to myself.

I called Ms. Lenora and requested she book my plane

tickets and lodging in New Orleans for Thanksgiving. When she asked the requisite question of why, I gave her the educational aspects of New Orleans, from its history, its industry, and I added a sentimentality to my request by saying I just wanted to be in the South for a while, because I hadn't been there since my mother's funeral. She immediately made the arrangements. Part one of my plan was going accordingly. Bishop covers pawn.

# 10

# 11:59:22

I wonder if folks remember when they first caught sight of their home. Of the place where they felt as if they'd always belonged. I wonder if they remember the feeling which flowed through their souls then. Everyone dreams of such a place, but too often we settle for places which don't inspire those feelings, places foisted on us by others, where we never feel totally comfortable. Home is where the heart is, and our souls let us know when we've found the place our hearts have yearned to live.

My hotel was located in the French Quarter of New Orleans, and as my taxi from the airport drove me towards my destination, my head was on a swivel, taking in everything I could. The scent from the magnolia blossoms were alluring, as was the gentle November breeze, but the city itself seemed to be whispering to me, "Welcome Home." The hustle and bustle of living here seemed to have a rhythm to it, a vibe I'd never experienced before in any other place, including Mississippi. Everything moved with an easy pace here, or so it seemed to my sixteen-year-old eyes.

My taxi dropped me off at a swanky hotel located in the heart of the Quarter. Even at two in the afternoon, it seemed as if there was a party going on everywhere. The brass sounds of the street bands seemed to all be playing in cadence, the added tapping of the little boys dancing in their homemade tap shoes contributed to a funky, fulfilling sound unlike any music heard anywhere.

I quickly checked into my room, hurrying onto the adjoining balcony in order to view this melting pot of a city. From my balcony I observed mimes, dancers, vendors, tourists, and street musicians, dancing, singing, and creating a revelry which is unique to New Orleans. I now understood the meaning of the city's nickname, The Big Easy. Everything blended together so easily, so seamlessly, much like a dish I tried for the first time later on, gumbo. Gumbo is a dish based loosely on French bouillabaisse, but it's a blending of different flavors and different cultures, more truly representative of New Orleans than any other dish or product, except maybe jazz.

The first day there, I wandered around the French Quarter until the sun started to set. I had a shrimp po' boy on St. Peter's, a bowl of seafood gumbo on Chartres, and

I had a humorous picture of myself drawn at Jackson Square by a street artist. I walked around intoxicated for the rest of the day, drunk on the culture I'd witnessed firsthand, not out of a book. I sat on my balcony after sunset, watching the reveling from my thirsty perch. I was amazed and inspired by the city, and I found myself daydreaming about being a part of it all.

I arose early the next morning, impatient to see what I could discover. A kid in a candy store is the only description of myself which can give an idea of how I felt. Before I left my hotel, I appraised myself in the mirror. I was six feet tall, with a beginner's mustache, I was dressed nicely, and I had money. Basically, I didn't look sixteen, at least not to me.

Beignets at the famous Café Du Monde were a must, accompanied by chicory coffee, and that was my breakfast for the day. I did other touristy type things that morning, such as riding the St. Charles streetcar, exploring the Riverwalk, and by mid-afternoon I'd worn myself out. I hadn't taken any cabs, choosing to walk everywhere, in order to feel the pulse of the city for myself. I stumbled to my hotel room, where I opened the balcony doors to let in the atmosphere, and I passed out, sleeping like a rock, with the rhythmic noises of Bourbon Street serving as a lullaby. I woke later in the evening, thirsty and hungry. It was past sunset, but I wasn't too worried. I'd stay within running distance of the hotel, in case trouble occurred. I dressed carefully, knowing the way I dressed would be an important part of my plan.

I ate dinner at the first restaurant I encountered. I devoured a meal consisting of shrimp étoufée, French bread, and I ordered a beer, just to see what would happen. They served me with no problem, and the first beer of my life was an ice cold Bud. I finished my dinner, then I steeled my nerves for my next test of the night.

A couple of doors down from the restaurant where I'd eaten dinner there was a smoke-filled bar, featuring a live band, and three-for-one drink specials. I entered the establishment and sidled up to the bar as if I'd done it a million times. The bartender met my eyes, and I ordered a Rémy Martin on the rocks and a Bud. The bartender's head tilted to the side as he sized me up, trying to gauge if I was old enough. I kept my face impassive, as if ordering a drink was something I did all of the time. Finally, after what seemed like eons, he nodded to me, and as he turned to fetch my drinks, I let out the breath I'd been holding.

After he returned with my drinks I sat at the bar, sipping my cognac, and marveling at the spirit of this city. I hadn't been questioned about my age, which was a fine piece of luck. Maybe the bartender knew I was underage and didn't care. Or maybe he'd been sixteen once and remembered sneaking his first drink. Whatever the case, I would not look a gift horse in the mouth. I would be mature as possible, and even though I knew enough to pace my drinking, I think the vibe of New Orleans had infected me with some kind of "good time" disease. I think the disease was known as *Laissez les bon temps rouler*. The English translation is simply *Let the good times roll.*

I fell in love that day, not with a woman, but with a place. New Awlins, NOLA, the Big Easy, whatever name you wanted to call it. I loved New Orleans from first sight, and I vowed it would be my home as soon as I finished with Boniface. As the bartender poured my second and third rounds of drinks, I was trying to decide which university in New Orleans I'd be attending when a sultry voice asked me, "Is someone sitting here or are you waiting for someone?"

I snapped out of my reverie to appraise the young woman who'd asked the question. She stood maybe five-foot-three, coal black hair, alabaster skin, and slight curves encased in a short black skirt, with a matching bustier, a short jacket, and high heels. She was pretty and attractive, but not beautiful, at least not traditionally so.

"No, I'm not waiting for anyone, or saving the seat, unless I was waiting for you and I didn't know it," I said. Kind of lame, but she smiled and sat on the stool next to me. My insides quivered and my loins moaned, as she slid sinuously onto the stool. She offered me a brilliant smile, and I almost lost whatever vestiges of coolness I may have had.

In the deepest voice I could muster, I tremulously introduced myself to my new friend. "Everyone calls me Jackson," I said. "Can I draft you as a drinking partner? My treat."

She smiled at me, nodded her head in assent, then she extended her soft hand towards me. "Since we're going to be drinking partners, my name is Alicia," she said. "I'll have whatever you're drinking, and you can keep me entertained." Her hand was clasped in mine, the contrast between our skin tones both alluring and different. Her fingernails were short and manicured, painted in fire engine red. Alicia's hand in mine was the first feminine touch of someone other than my mama or grandmother.

As I ordered another round, the band began to play a bluesy number about a brown-eyed girl. Alicia's eyes were reminiscent of lightly creamed coffee, mesmerizing to a neophyte such as myself. As the band played, I had my first conversation with a member of the fairer sex. The band's songs served both as a soundtrack for our conversation, and as subject matter. Alicia and I discussed the meanings and possible origins of the ideas for the songs being played. As the band played on, the fine elixir produced by champagne grapes constantly lubricated our throats, making me somewhat carefree and loquacious.

A couple of hours later, my limit was reached. Attempting to dance, I stumbled into Alicia, causing the bartender to inform me I was finished drinking for the evening. I nodded in comprehension, quickly pulling out cash to settle my tab. Looking at Alicia, I reviewed all we had discussed since she'd sat on the stool next to me. We'd discussed music, poetry, art, and I'd even attempted to converse in my newly learned French. Neither of us had offered any personal information other than our names, but I knew I wasn't ready to end this date, or whatever it was.

As I gave the bartender a well deserved tip, I carefully weighed the words I needed to convey to Alicia. I needed to be cool, yet direct, but I didn't want to offend her nor scare her off.

"Would you be interested in accompanying me to my hotel room?" I asked. "It's nearby, and maybe we can continue our conversation, or maybe even find other pursuits with which to amuse ourselves."

Alicia smiled in the seductive manner which had been luring men to jump ships, abandon dreams, and leap into abysses since the beginning of time. She nodded at me knowingly, and arm in arm, we exited the bar.

I floated down the street, the cognac providing a pleasantly tipsy cushion, shielding me from the reality of what was happening. I was strolling down Bourbon Street, accompanied by a sweet- smelling temptress on the way to my hotel where, hopefully, I'd take another step on my path to manhood. Romantic, whimsical thoughts flooded my brain. I'd already made my decision to attend college in New Orleans, and my alcohol addled brain was trying to find a place for Alicia in my future here. As a girlfriend, confidante, or Pen Pal, I didn't know which, but in my naiveté I knew I needed to fit her into my life. When floating along in a daydream, all things seem possible.

Alicia helped guide me to my hotel room, steering me up the stairs and to my room. I seemed to have sobered up somewhat, maybe the enormity of the situation was overwhelming the effects of the cognac. The precipice of which I'd dreamt was so close I could taste it.

After closing the door to the room, I stared into Alicia's eyes, unsure of my next move. None of the books I'd read had prepared me for the proper moves which would lead to the ultimate horizontal dance. I hesitated briefly, before throwing caution to the wind. I leaned in, clumsily embracing Alicia as I attempted to kiss her. She averted her mouth so my questing kiss landed on the side of her face. She raised her hand to my chest, stopping me in my tracks. Puzzled and nervous, I waited for her explanation, fear rising in my chest. So close.

"Jackson, I'm really enjoying your company and the conversation, so I'm willing to give you a discount," Alicia said. "I usually get three hundred dollars a night per customer, especially for an all-night date. However, since I'm pretty sure this is your first time, I'll only charge you a hundred for tonight, especially considering this has been a wonderful date. It's up to you."

I was dumbfounded, feeling as if someone had thrown a bucket of ice water over my romantic visions. Damn. The first woman I would have sex with was a professional. I weighed my options for maybe five seconds before nodding, and reaching for my wallet. As I was counting out one hundred dollars, Alicia began to disrobe. I laid the money on the top of the dresser, and I turned to Alicia. She guided my mouth to her bared, round breast, and I sucked upon her nipple like a starving man.

During the course of the night, Alicia made love to me at least five times. I feasted upon her breasts, squeezing her soft places, and discovered the reason why men go insane over women. I used the condoms which every teenaged boy carries with him on his person, in case of emergency or opportunity. I definitely got my money's worth from Alicia. As we lay there sweating, I had an epiphany. I had a few more days to be in New Orleans, and I did have money. I whispered my proposition into Alicia's ear, and she assented to my proposal after only a few seconds.

If anyone has been paying attention to my thought process up to that point, they would know what my proposal was. I've shown myself as the consummate student, gobbling up life lessons on my journey. I offered Alicia a hundred dollars a night to make love with me, as well as to teach me the finer points of lovemaking. I wanted to know which spots on a woman's body were the most sensitive, which things to avoid, and which moves would drive a woman crazy with desire. I spent the rest of my Thanksgiving break learning things to help me succeed with future quests. I won't go too much in detail, because I'd hate to give away too much too soon.

At the end of my vacation I hugged Alicia, gave her a hefty tip, and I made sure I had her pertinent information, such as her phone number. Alicia confessed she'd enjoyed our time together as much as I had. She said she wouldn't be averse to seeing me again, saying I'd been a welcome vacation from her reality.

I'll give one guess as to where I spent my Christmas vacation. I went right back to New Orleans, where I continued to enjoy the lustful lessons taught to me by a professional.

# 11

# 11:59:24

Athletes get paid what the market allows, and I don't have a problem with the money they make. Teachers are woefully underpaid, but theirs is an honorable and respected profession, and their employers do not make a profit based on their skills. Prostitutes, however, are not appreciated and are shunned by respectable society. I have never understood why, because they provide a needed service. If the illegality of prostitution is based on morals, then alcohol, tobacco, and other vices should be illegal as well, considering they cause much more damage than prostitution. Imagine how the economy would respond if prostitution were legalized in all fifty states, taxed and regulated accordingly. Just one of those thoughts which plague me in the wee hours of the morning, when my brain refuses to rest.

When I returned to Boniface after Christmas, my attitude was noticeably different. I felt as if my classmates were a bunch of spoiled brats, with no idea of the harsh realities of the world. Yet they had the nerve, gall, and audacity to disdain me based on my skin being darker than theirs. Their dislike of me wasn't based on my behavior, my intellect, or my skill set. They disliked me because I was Black, and others had told them it was all right to feel that way. Well, fuck them, and I was through turning the other cheek. I would give no quarter and no mercy for my last semester at Boniface. They'd put me through unnecessary turmoil, forcing me to deal with undeserved rancor for close to four years. I had arrived at Boniface, a grieving, naïve boy, dealing with probably the most painful event any young boy had ever dealt with, and none of them had ever been through the things I'd lived through. My classmates had piled an awful lot of hurt on top of the burdens I already carried, and their ringleader had constantly egged them on. Payback time was coming.

Since I'd been at Boniface I'd learned how to play chess, how to manage money, how to speak multiple foreign languages, and how to make love to a woman. I'd also learned how to suffer in silence, how to revel in being unique, and how ignorance can overwhelm common sense. Common sense isn't all that common, to be honest.

I called Ms. Lenora once the semester started, to

update her on my college plans. I informed her I would be attending Tulane University in the fall. I had submitted applications to Tulane, Xavier, LSU, and Dillard universities. Tulane not only accepted me, they were offering me a full scholarship for four years. Something inside of me told me to keep the scholarship information to myself. I told Ms. Lenora how much the tuition and housing would cost for four years. She informed me Bobby Jr. would be apprised of the situation and he'd respond to me personally. He and I had normally communicated through Ms. Lenora, so I was a bit wary.

A week or so later, I received a thick envelope from Bobby Jr. The three-page letter enclosed informed me he had deposited four years of tuition money into my account, plus living expenses. He further stated he had fulfilled his moral obligation to me by ensuring my education was taken care of. I learned in the letter I'd receive more money on my eighteenth birthday, from rents and leases on my grandmother's land, of which I was the owner. He'd included the paperwork for my properties and my bank account, with the most recent balances. Basically, he was cutting the purse strings, leaving me to sink or swim on my own.

The irony to me was I'd been on my own since I'd gotten on the train to come north. Sure, Bobby Jr. paid for my education and lifestyle, but he was supposed to. Fathers do it all the time. I discovered my strengths, I molded them, and I furthered myself without a daddy or a loving mentor. I'd be fine by myself going forward because the money in the bank allowed me the freedom to be me, no matter who I ended up becoming.

I'd been given $250,000, earmarked for college. But the scholarship meant I could save that money, and I'd just transfer it from the account to another one of my own creation. As I looked at my balances, I made a vow to never be in the position to have to ask anyone for anything ever again. Not love, comfort, or understanding. I didn't need it and I wouldn't beg for it. Or so I thought then.

College was taken care of, my future finances were secure, leaving me with only one unsettled bit of business at Boniface—revenge. With all of my affairs in order, I could focus on my next move.

Lars Nicholls Jr. was going to attend Notre Dame in the fall, and I didn't see our paths crossing again once we graduated. A checkers player would have played a nasty prank on him, tried to have sex with his girlfriend, or kicked his ass. But I'm a chess player, and I knew any of those actions wouldn't leave a permanent mark upon him. At least not as deep as the scars he'd inflicted upon me. His girlfriend was a typically blond, preppy snob, and banging her probably would have disgusted me. Even if I'd knocked him off of his pedestal in some public way, his followers would have propped him right back up. My revenge needed to be as private as it could be, in order to push the hurt deep into his soul.

Octavia Nicholls was a redheaded Irish woman from the south side of Chicago. Her scholarship to Notre Dame as a recipient of their Scholar's Award had been mentioned in the neighborhood newspaper where she'd grown up. All of the information about her was easily found on the Internet. From her birth as Octavia Patricia

Sullivan forty years before, to details of her wedding to Lawrence Nicholls Sr., and her eventual emergence as a successful romance novelist, writing under the pseudonym Tavia Sullivan. The information was so easily obtained, I didn't even print it out. I could just log in and find out whatever I needed.

As the wife of a wealthy industrialist, Mrs. Nicholls sat on several boards in the region. She was the chairwoman for the fundraising committee for Boniface, meaning she'd always be present at parties and dinners. I even read a couple of her novels, trying to learn as much about her as I could. In the pictures of her on the Internet her husband was rarely pictured with her, which gave me food for thought. Lars was the only child of their union, and as I learned more about her public persona, I didn't see the attraction of her husband. She was a butterfly married to a turtle, in my eyes. She even spoke French. As the Sweethearts Dance approached, I knew as much about her as was available to the public. Anything further would have to be learned and discovered first-hand.

The annual Sweethearts Dance was the last fundraiser of the year at Boniface. It always took place a week before spring break, and formal attire was required. The girls from a nearby private school attended this function as well, but this time, none of them were a concern of mine. I had a much richer prize in mind. I studied formal wear trends, and I decided to take the train to Chicago to acquire the duds I'd need.

I had no problem locating the clothes I needed in the city. A traditional tuxedo, but I eschewed a cummerbund for a vest with flecks of emerald on it. A matching tie, shirt, and black shoes completed my ensemble. On a whim I called Ms. Lenora, requesting she book a room for me in downtown Chicago for spring break. She assured me it wouldn't be a problem, before reminding me I was responsible for my own finances. I acknowledged her concern, then I asked her if she would continue to handle my business for me, outside of her duties for Bobby Jr. My request took her by surprise, and we negotiated for a few minutes. We agreed upon compensation on an as-needed basis, and I faxed her a rudimentary nondisclosure agreement and a contract. She sent everything back to me quite speedily, and I had my first employee, even though I'd never met her. Until I finished college Ms. Lenora would handle my business and expenses. Yet my mistrust of Bobby Jr. kept me from ever letting Ms. Lenora know everything I was doing. I kept my left hand blind as to the moves of my right hand. Chess.

I entered the Sweethearts Dance about an hour after it started, due to wanting to make a noticeable entrance. I timed it just right, because the receiving line was over, and I was free to move around at my leisure. The young ladies whom I'd attempted to chat up back in the fall made eye contact, some even smiled invitingly, but I was way past their level. I didn't want to play around with tittering little girls. I was intrigued by women—one in particular.

The room was decorated nicely, refreshment tables on two sides of the room. A band was playing soft rock, ballads mostly, and there were a few couples dancing. My eyes leisurely swept the room, a patient panther waiting for my prey. A flash of deep red hair drew my attention, and there she was, obliterating every other female in the vicinity. Emerald green gown, one shoulder exposed, matching emerald heels, and a smile which lit up the dark places inside of me.

As the night progressed I kept her in sight, without staring or approaching her. Attempting to play it cool, I waited for my opportunity. When Mrs. Nicholls separated from a crowd of people, she made a beeline towards the punch bowl. And I pounced.

"*Bonjour*, Madame Nicholls," I said. She looked up in surprise, then smiled as she apparently remembered me.

"*Bonjour jeune homme. Parlez-vous français?*" she asked.

"*Je parle un peu français*, but I'm still way more fluent in English," I said.

She laughed and her laughter was reminiscent of the sweetest love song ever heard, the song which provided the soundtrack for all of one's daydreams.

"I am practicing my French because my graduation gift is a Parisian vacation. I need to at least be somewhat understandable so I won't be dismissed as a typical American," I said. "It'll be my first trip to Paris, and I'm trying to find out where the best places to eat are. I have an idea about where I'll stay, but I don't want to be confused or lost while I'm there."

She smiled at me knowingly. "Paris is one of my favorite cities in the world, but I think you knew that already. Next you'll tell me you've read one of my books, in an attempt to flatter me. I'm impressed already, Jackson. Why don't you meet me for lunch next Tuesday and bring your notebook?"

"Wow, I'm honored, Mrs. Nicholls, but I'll be in Chicago for Spring Break. Is it possible you could meet me there?" I asked, wide-eyed. I was attempting to come off as a harmless puppy, as opposed to a prowling wolf.

Her eyes twinkled with laughter, and she seemed to appraise me with a different sort of look on her face. She opened up her small evening bag and withdrew a business card. She handed the card to me, and I hurriedly put it in the inside pocket of my tuxedo.

"I think I'll drive to the city to do some shopping on Michigan Avenue. Call me around nine or so on Tuesday, and we can meet for lunch. I need to make my rounds now," she said. "Don't forget your notebook."

Mrs. Nicholls walked away to talk to other guests, and I looked around the room for Lars. He was sipping punch in a corner, talking to his ditzy girlfriend. Good, he hadn't witnessed the two-minute conversation between his mother and me. I left the party soon after, making my way to my solitary dorm room. As I hung up my tuxedo, thoughts of Mrs. Nicholls would not let me sleep, and I wondered whose king was in danger—mine or hers?

# 12

# 11:59:25

I've read theories about love and falling in love. I read a theory a person will fall in love with the same exact person over and over again, but maybe just not in the same body. Same soul, different form. Interesting theory, and I can see the validity of theories such as that one. Every woman a man will ever fall for will have vestiges of someone they once loved. Maybe so. Or maybe love itself is a bullshit theory designed to keep us from seeing the truth about the myth of life. Life is pain, and moments of happiness are just anesthesia to dull the pain of living. Cynicism is both a gift and a curse.

I spent the first day of my spring break in Chicago

touring and revisiting the most famous museums in the city: The Art Institute, the Field Museum of History, the Shedd Aquarium, and the Adler Planetarium. The museums were all located close together, within walking distance, making it easy for the average tourist to see all of them on the same day, unlike other cities where the museums are across town from one another.

On Tuesday morning I woke at the ass crack of dawn, impatient for my lunch date with Mrs. Nicholls. In all of my so-called scheming and plotting, I hadn't thought of what I'd actually say to her when the time came. "Yes, I'd like to fuck you as the ultimate act of revenge against your assboil of a son." Even though there was truth in the statement, I don't think it would have been a good idea, nor a classy move. Whatever the reasons for my actions, I did not want to appear crass to her, because she was not the target of my revenge.

I ordered breakfast but I only nibbled at it, my stomach feeling as if it were full of drunken butterflies. Around 9:15 I called the number on the business card Mrs. Nicholls had given me. When the voice-mail came on, I hurriedly left the name of my downtown hotel, plus the time I'd meet her in the restaurant downstairs. I hung up, feeling drained, as if I'd just ran a marathon. I needed to calm myself down.

I turned on the radio, letting the music help with my nerves. I took a long relaxing shower, singing along with the radio as I luxuriated in the steamy mist. I was remarkably calmer a little while later as I got dressed. Looking in the mirror at my freshly-scrubbed reflection, I acknowledged to myself I was still a kid, no matter how free my lifestyle was. My trysts with Alicia in New Orleans had been paid transactions with a woman only a couple of years older than me. It had been Little League compared to what I was facing. Maybe I wasn't ready yet, but it was too late to give in to those worries.

Once downstairs I let the hostess seat me at a table for two, towards the back of the restaurant. I ordered a glass of lemonade, which I sipped as I nervously watched the entrance. What if she didn't show? Then all of my research and maneuvers would have been for nothing. I didn't see us meeting again in the course of my remaining time at Boniface, meaning this dream of revenge would go unfulfilled.

At ten minutes after noon I requested a menu and another lemonade from the hovering waiter, just to give us both something to do. I pretended to peruse the menu, but in reality all of the words were just dark blurs upon the page.

"Did you order me a lemonade as well?" she asked.

I was startled as I looked up at her, wondering how I hadn't noticed her approach. The scent of her perfume should have been enough to alert me to her presence. Chanel Number Five, I found out later. Classy, vintage perfume for a mature and elegant woman. Suddenly, all of the words and lines I'd practiced disappeared from my brain, leaving me unsure and unready.

The waiter pulled her chair out for her, and she ordered a Scotch neat after she was seated. Mrs. Nicholls smiled at me, and suddenly, I felt like the prey.

"Did you bring your notebook?" she asked.

The waiter returned with her drink, and she looked at

me over the rim as she sipped. There was a gold chain around her neck, and the small medallion of a unicorn seemed to be serving its purpose of drawing attention to the lush, roundness of her cleavage. I felt my heart beating in my ears.

"It's upstairs," I stammered, unsure of where she was going with this conversation.

"Pity, I can only stay for a little while, because I have a pressing engagement I must attend. And as much as I'd enjoy watching you stammer and stutter for awhile, I just don't have the time. I'm sure you understand." She finished her drink, then waved to the waiter for another Scotch. "We'll have to reschedule for another time."

I was crestfallen, but what could I say? My so-called plans were lying in ruins, and I struggled to think of something to say. "I'd like to reschedule for another day. I'll be here all week." My words sounded weak and pleading to my own ears. "Just let me know when to call. I'll probably just go to the movies or something."

"Is that what you really wanted to do with me? Take me to the movies? From the way you look at me, I would think something much more intimate is in your thoughts," she said. "How can someone know you're hungry or thirsty for something if you never speak of it? For a handsome, charming young man, there's still a lot you need to learn. Well, you know what they say—when the student is ready, the master will appear."

I didn't know what to say or what to do. My brain was stuck in neutral, and I could not decipher whether or not she'd admitted her reciprocity about there possibly being something between us, or if she was making fun of my attraction to her. If we were playing chess, I'd have understood immediately. Or rather chess on a board, because I think we were having a different kind of chess match.

"It's always good to have a backup plan," Mrs. Nicholls said. "I do need a favor, though. I need to freshen up and make a phone call. May I borrow your room key? I shouldn't be more than twenty minutes. Just give me a few minutes, then you can get the key when you come up."

Speechless, I slid my hand into my pants pocket and handed her my key. She rose and walked in the direction of the bank of elevators. I watched her walk away, her gait slow and rhythmic, knowing my window of opportunity had probably just closed. Dejected, appetite completely gone, I signaled for the waiter, and I requested the check. I assured him everything was fine, I just wasn't hungry anymore. A few minutes later, I paid the check, leaving the waiter a nice tip. He had been quite attentive in fulfilling his few duties.

The best laid plans often go awry, I know. In war and off the battlefield, the best of plans rarely survive first contact with the opposing force. Mine surely hadn't. I walked toward the elevator, replaying our conversation in my mind, trying to figure out where I'd gone wrong. I had always prided myself on being calm, cool, and collected, but I'd failed. As the elevator rose to my floor, I could only hope I'd get another chance to see Mrs. Nicholls before spring break ended.

My room was toward the end of the hall to the left of the elevators. As I walked, a thought occurred to me suddenly. Why hadn't she freshened up in one of the washrooms in the lobby? I raised my hand to knock on the door of my room, number 1159, and I noticed the door was ajar. I pushed it open slowly and stepped in.

"Mrs. Nicholls?" I said, stepping through the door and closing it softly behind me. I took a few steps into the room, thinking I must have been coming up in the elevator as she was going down. Seeds of disappointment settled even further into my psyche as my eyes swept the room, which still smelled of her Chanel Number Five.

"I think at this point, you can call me Octavia," Mrs. Nicholls, or rather Octavia, said.

Octavia was lying naked in my bed, her clothes folded neatly on the chair. She'd been hinting at our mutual attraction, but the message had gone unheeded. Well, at least now I knew. Her coral-tipped breasts seemed to be calling to me, her reddish pubic hairs glistening in anticipation. My mouth watered and my penis rose to new heights. Stiff-legged, I walked towards the bed, dazzled and mesmerized by the lush beauty of her. She lifted her hand towards me, and I joined my hand to hers, willing to let her orchestrate the scene, all thoughts of Lars gone from my head.

"Time to take notes," she said, before guiding my face gently to the curly red thatch at the apex of her thighs.

As I placed a soft kiss upon her sex, a vision ran through my mind of a king being laid on its side, an admission of defeat in the game of chess. Then my thoughts turned carnal, and the oldest game in the history of the world began to be played.

# 13

# 11:59:26

Throughout life, in order to be successful, one must be willing to learn. There's a lesson to be learned every day of our existence, whether a simple lesson or a complex one. When the pupil is ready, the teacher will appear. In my life I have been the consummate student, always striving to get better, to learn more. My most painful lessons always revolved around the same subject—love. Love is the most complex, most painful subject a human being can learn or experience. In love, there are teachers and pupils, but there are no masters.

On a magical Tuesday afternoon I used my mouth, hands, and my throbbing manhood in ways I hadn't been taught by Alicia. Every time I used my mouth to kiss Octavia's most intimate cavern, she kissed me voraciously afterward, as if she couldn't get enough of tasting herself. I couldn't get enough of her, and comparing the lovemaking we shared to my Alicia experience was akin to comparing a burger to a steak. Over a nine-hour span, we made love five times. During interludes, she teased me a bit about the look on my face when she had risen from the table. Octavia told me I needed to work on keeping a poker face, which would help me keep my reactions to myself. She said she could read my interest in her on my face the first time we'd met. I jotted her words down in my mental notebook.

A first lovemaking session between two people is fraught with hesitancy, as explorations and discoveries happen rapidly. It's natural, but by the third or fourth round sexual compatibility takes over, removing inhibitions. I learned her likes and dislikes, storing them in my mental database, hoping this wouldn't be a one-time affair.

Octavia asked if I'd spend the remaining days of my vacation with her. I quickly acquiesced, yet a feeling of guilt remained. I'd achieved my so-called revenge by sleeping with her, but I hadn't factored her in as a human being. I liked her, and now using her seemed petty and somewhat childish. There was no sense of achievement or vindication. It felt more as if I were on the verge of a great adventure with Octavia as a guide and sidekick. I was tempted to tell her my revenge motivation to see how she would respond. Instead, I asked how her husband would feel about her being gone all week. Her response and subsequent story took me by surprise.

"My husband lives his life, and I live mine, both of us treating each other with respect, but not love or affection. He and our son are fishing in the Upper Peninsula of Michigan this week, but even if he weren't gone, my absence would not upset him," she said. Then she began to unburden herself of the tale of her marriage to Lawrence Nicholls Sr. I listened with mouth agape, fascinated by her tale.

During her senior year at Notre Dame she'd met her future husband at a poetry reading. He'd been charming, handsome, and interesting, and they began to date. Octavia was an Irish girl from Chicago, so Lawrence's world of country clubs, formal parties, and money was fascinating to her. The things in his world were things of which she'd only read about in magazines or books, adding more attraction to him, making him seem a worthier prize.

"I began to daydream of the life I could have being his wife," she said. "My view of life at the time was rose colored, not allowing me to see the picture clearly. Be careful what you wish for, because your wish may come true."

One night, the soon to be graduated Octavia had been at a formal event with Lawrence. The alcohol flowed freely, and Lawrence drank like a man dying of thirst. Afterward in his car, a routine petting session of kissing and groping morphed into a nightmare. Up until that night, he'd been respectful of her Catholic upbringing and her virginity. He raped her in his car, ignoring her pleas to stop or the repeated use of the word "No." They had still been parked in the country club's parking lot. Afterward, with no apology given, he drove her back to campus and dropped her off.

I had ordered room service for us, prior to the beginning of her story, because food was needed. Especially since I hadn't eaten anything all day.

"I didn't tell anyone. I didn't call the police or alert any of my friends. I willed myself to move on from him," Octavia continued. She was sitting up in the bed, the bedcovers wrapped around her. "I made the easy decision to not answer his phone calls, and to leave his letters unopened. He'd taken something which was only mine to give. I never forgave him."

"Then how'd you end up married to him?" I asked. "Especially after he raped you."

"Because the world was a different place then," she said. "Two months later, after days of vomiting and headaches, I found out I was pregnant. I confronted Lawrence with my diagnosis and his father and my parents insisted we get married. We had a small wedding, just our close friends and family. Life happens and you deal with it as best you can, and if it means sacrificing dreams and goals, you do what you have to in that moment."

She was interrupted by a knock on the door. I opened the door for room service, tipped him, and then I rolled the cart in myself. I could tell food wasn't on either of our minds just then. I climbed back in the bed with her, and lay my hand upon hers. Something was happening which I couldn't quite put my finger on.

"Isn't it crazy how one event can shape the rest of our

lives?" I asked. "Were you able to move forward in your marriage, despite the way it began? Because you've been married a long time."

"Yes, I have been married for a long time. After Lars was born, I tried to make a go of it. We went on dates, vacations, we really tried. The lovemaking part of it was lackluster, but we tried. We appeared to all eyes to be a perfect young family." Her voice sounded wistful, as if she had longed for the realization of the American Dream.

"But then, it was all destroyed in a heartbeat. The baby was a little crabby, so I slept in the nursery most nights. One night I went downstairs to get a glass of water, and I heard something in the den," she said. "Curious, I went to check the noise out. Opening the door slowly, I watched in horrified amazement as our chauffeur Pierre and my husband had sex. I watched for a few moments, my body numbed into a state of shock. I quietly exited the room eventually. I knew suddenly why he'd raped me. Lawrence had assaulted me to prove his masculinity to himself. I waited a couple of days, then I confronted him. He tearfully admitted to his homosexuality and from then on, our marriage was in name only."

I hugged her to me, amazed at the story she'd told, wondering at her strength. As we sat there, with me idly stroking her long red hair, unconsciously I began to whisper a story into her ear. A story of a little boy whose mother was killed while he listened. I told her of the trials and tribulations the little boy faced in a world where no one loved him. She turned to me, tears streaking her face, and hugged me fiercely.

"Never give up on love," she murmured into my ear.

"Never."

A little while later, a thought crossed my mind as we lay in each other's arms. I knew my reasons for being there with her, but I was lost as to why she was really here with me. I broke the companionable silence with a question which my curiosity wouldn't let me keep to myself.

"Why me?" I asked. "What was it about me that resulted in us being here like this?"

Octavia pulled slightly away from me, a puzzled look on her face. Then a smile burst across her face, and she gave me a soft kiss upon the lips before answering.

"I gave up part of my youth to become an unwanted and unwelcome wife. Then one evening at a boring dance, a tall, dark, and charming young man struck up a conversation with me. I was flattered, intrigued, and I admit, a little bit turned on by the young man's attention. I felt a slight bit of guilt over your age, but the more I'm around you, I'm becoming aware you're wise and mature beyond your years. I am glad you had the nerve to approach me, and I'm happy I took the chance. I don't know where we're going to go with this thing we've started, but I'm going to enjoy every minute of it. You might not realize it, but you've brought sunshine and smiles to a dark and lonely existence. Thank you."

We slept like two spoons in a drawer, hugging each other while dreams flitted through our heads. Two survivors clinging to each other. When I woke the next morning, her head upon my chest, I was overcome with a stunning realization. Out of my plans for revenge, something strangely wonderful was born. As I kissed her forehead gently I felt something new, something unforeseen. I had finally made a connection with another human being.

My grandmother Lily and my mama Flora Jean had been the only people I'd ever been close to, or with whom I'd had any kind of camaraderie. I had missed my chance to form a friendship with Jerry, and my status as an outcast, pariah, and outsider at Boniface prevented anyone else from even attempting to get to know me. I stroked Octavia's hair, thinking of the love, laughter, and secrets we'd shared. Being her lover was wondrous of course, but my soul rejoiced even more with a different realization—I finally had a friend.

# 14

# 11:59:27

There are certain periods of our lives we wish we could revisit, and just live there. Everyone has enjoyed a Golden Era in their own lives when everything was perfect, but, of course, none of us realized it then. The grass was greener, the sun seemed to shine brighter, and the world was a friendlier place. I'm sitting here now, wishing for a time machine. I'd revel in every minute, hour, day, and month of my own perfect era, never letting go.

My last spring break vacation in Chicago was idyllic, memorable, and romantic. We made love constantly, as we explored the depths of each other, physically and spiritually. The two of us played, laughed, and talked, with the city serving as our personal playground. Octavia unchained the hidden depths of myself I had previously been unaware of, and I unknowingly gave her a canvas on which to paint her own needs and desires.

In our conversations we talked of politics, sports, my parents, literature, food, and traveling. I confessed my desire to see as much of the world as time allowed, starting after graduation. Octavia's response surprised and enthused me.

"You mentioned traveling to Paris after graduation. Why don't you let me take you to Europe for the summer? Consider it a graduation gift."

I was shocked and thrilled, and I agreed immediately. Octavia said she'd take care of everything, all I needed to do was to be prepared with my luggage and passport. We'd leave the day after graduation, not to return until my orientation at Tulane.

On our last evening we had dinner in a restaurant overlooking Lake Michigan. We'd become so close in such a short period of time, I felt I owed her an explanation for everything.

"This thing between us has blown me away," I said. "In all of my imaginings, I never saw this coming. When I saw you I was immediately attracted to you, but once I found out who you were, I thought of how much pain your son has inflicted on me, and I thought you might be the pathway to my own sort of revenge. Those plans and thoughts have been thrown in the garbage, never to be mentioned by me again. But I am glad I pursued you."

"I suspected something, but I was nevertheless

flattered. I think I'll enjoy our relationship, and I don't think you need to throw this in my son's face. Ever. Especially since I think this will be good for both of us," Octavia said.

"When I started my pursuit of you, it was because of who you are to my enemy," I said. "Now that you're truly in my life as both lover and friend, the revenge part no longer exists for me. The past is in the past, and the future is looking bright. I want to keep you in my life and to do so, I have to keep our relationship a secret. Keeping secrets is not a problem for me, especially one as beautiful and delicious as you."

When I returned to Boniface nothing bothered me. I floated through those last two months laughing at the comments of my enemies, secure in the knowledge it was almost over. When Lars would make one of his racial remarks, I'd ignore them pitying him because I knew his back story. He was the spoiled son of two parents trapped in a loveless marriage due to his existence. The noble part of me felt sorry for the bastard, while the petty part of me smirked inwardly, knowing I'd already been sexually intimate with his mother, and would be again soon.

In the days before graduation I stripped my room bare, throwing things away, packing up my belongings, readying myself for my exit from this place. I remembered Jerry wistfully for a moment, lamenting a missed opportunity. I wouldn't miss Boniface in the least. It had been a terrible experience for the most part, but I was somewhat grateful for the experience, good and bad.

The graduation ceremony went according to schedule—no surprises. As each graduate received his diploma, their university or armed forces branch was announced. Navy, Notre Dame, a couple of Ivy League schools, and a slew of others. I was the only one going to Tulane, which meant I wouldn't have to see any of those bastards again in life. I was neither the valedictorian nor the salutatorian, but it was fine with me. I had no regrets, and I'd graduated with honors.

After the ceremony, as graduates and their families milled around, I made eye contact with Octavia. She was standing next to her husband and son, but the look we shared conveyed our mutual desire to be on a plane.

I was standing there, daydreaming of foreign climes, when a tug on my sleeve snapped me out of my reverie. A woman of around forty-five years-old was standing in front of me, grinning from ear to ear. I was puzzled as to why this strange woman was smiling at me. She was pretty and slim, her short hairstyle drawing attention to her beautiful hazel eyes. I waited to hear what she had to say.

"I just had to make it my business to say something to you," she said, her voice reminiscent of the South, vaguely familiar. "You'll do fine at Tulane, but make sure to enjoy yourself. Be proud of your accomplishments. Enjoy your summer."

She patted me reassuringly on my shoulder, then turned and walked away, leaving me puzzled and bewildered. I wondered for a minute who she was and what her comments meant, but I had other things to think about. My train was leaving in a couple of hours for Chicago. Octavia was meeting me the next day, and we were flying to London, the first stop of my summer vacation.

On the plane the next day, Octavia talked to me about not wasting opportunities. She explained to me how some things in life never happen again. This trip might be my only chance to go to Europe, so I should revel in it, experience whatever my heart desired, and make enough memories to last a lifetime, because tomorrow isn't promised.

Did I take her advice to heart? Absolutely. London was a dream realized as we visited pubs daily, devouring fish and chips, of which I could not seem to get enough. I experienced the frenzy of Piccadilly Circus, and found myself giggling at the different British accents. On television all Brits seemed to sound exactly the same, but it's not true. Cockney accents, Oxford English, London slang, etc. They were all speaking the same language but the different nuances made it seem as if they weren't. It was fascinating to hear and witness.

At Westminster Abbey I stood in awe at Poets Corner, transfixed by the names of the writers and poets interred in that section of the Abbey. Chaucer, Browning, Kipling, and Dickens are just a few of the writers. There are also kings, queens, knights, and bishops buried there, which made me smirk as I thought of chessboard pieces. There were very few pawns there, unless one counted political victims. I was a book lover and a fan of history, and I felt blessed to have the opportunity to be in such a magnificent place.

Octavia was the ultimate tour guide, who made sure I saw the traditional tourist sights, as well as a few places off of the grid. We took a train north to Yorkshire, where we spent a weekend walking the moors, taking in the sights, and of course, making love as much as we wanted. Our two weeks in England flew by, and we discussed returning to the UK one day. We declared we'd visit Ireland, Wales, and Scotland, and instead of two weeks, we'd pend an entire month. It was a beautiful conversation, which animated our train ride to the Netherlands.

Amsterdam is a beautiful city, physically and spiritually. To this day I smile, remembering how it felt to sit at an outdoor café and smoke marijuana for the first time. Not just typical, homegrown weed, like one would find in America, but a whole menu of exotic, specially grown marijuana strains. I didn't become a fan of it, but I can see the allure of it, and I enjoyed watching Octavia indulge herself. It relaxes a person to an aware point of coolness, where they're okay with whatever is happening around them. I was under the spell of some kind of chocolate-flavored marijuana when Octavia took me on a tour of De Wallen, the most famous Red Light district in the world. An intricate outlay of women selling sex from behind transparent glass, showcasing every bit of their nakedness. It was an incredible sight to witness, especially for a goggle-eyed teenager.

I demurred on seeing and visiting the Anne Frank house. Knowing the history and outcome of her situation, I knew it would cast darkness over our trip. I chose instead to admire the tulips and the bicyclists, and the art which seemed to be everywhere. I chose light over darkness.

Paris. I'd dreamt of being in Paris ever since I was a

little kid, reading about D'Artagnan and his adventures there. My imagination hadn't come close to the reality—Paris was magical. We sipped wine and each other for two weeks. I experienced the Louvre, and the sheer beauty of the art displayed there. I was surprised by the miniscule size of the Mona Lisa painting, but the size was not important. Mona Lisa smiled at me, her secret little smile seeming to say she had many hidden layers to her, sort of like me, I realized. Octavia was pulling layer after layer off of the secret needs and desires I'd never shared with anyone. Every day I was with her, I became more and more vulnerable to something I hadn't allowed in my life for a long time—love.

We took a train from Paris to Rome, the seat of art and Christianity. Its art and history are on display throughout the city. I was awestruck by the ceiling at the Sistine Chapel, especially when the process of how it was created was explained. The genius of it was awe inspiring. My advice to someone lucky enough to get to Rome, is to not give themselves a timetable. It's best to leisurely explore and discover all of Rome, because one will be constantly astonished and amazed by the Spanish Steps, or the Colosseum, or Trevi Fountain. Incidentally, St. Peter's Basilica should be on everyone's bucket list, whether they are Catholic or not.

In Venice Octavia and I rode in a gondola, while the pilot of the boat sang sad love songs in Italian. She sat on my lap, in a sundress and sandals, smelling like all of the things which make a man's mouth water and his mind wonder. I kissed her then, softly, just to see if she tasted like a sinful daydream. As we kissed, the starlit night combined with the gondolier's voice, made it seem as if we were in a daydream. Later, we made love on the balcony of our room, teasing and tantalizing with our stroking, kissing, and caressing until the agony of our ecstasy shattered us both.

Venice was our last stop in that summer of discovery. Memorable in all ways, our European vacation is still painted vividly in my mind, over fifteen years later. I appreciated the advice Octavia had given me, about not wasting an opportunity. I hadn't. I experienced more in those two months than most people will probably experience in a lifetime. The saddest part of vacations is they all come to an end. Reality waits, a cruel reminder of the unknown which lies ahead.

We said farewell in the airport in Chicago with a heartfelt hug. We'd already made our plans for the future, as far as communicating and seeing each other. Phone calls and letters would suffice until she saw me for weekends or holidays. Octavia told me to embrace being in college, to drink the opportunities which would be in front of me. I promised her I would, because as I'd learned that magical summer, the banquet of life is a tempting feast of which everyone should eat until they're full.

# 15

# 11:59:28

When a fork in the road appears on the path of life, always take the rougher road to the desired destination. The journey is what makes the appreciation of achievement much greater. If everything one has ever wished for was handed to them on a silver platter, they'd have no appreciation for any of it. To get to one's desired destination, there need to be scars on their souls to remind them of all they have sacrificed and endured to make it to that point. People wear those scars proudly as proof of their perseverance.

As a scholarship student at Tulane University, I was required to maintain at least a 3.0 grade point average, and the terms required me to stay in a dormitory my first year. I remember thinking, *not that dorm shit again*, but it was different, completely different. I shared my room with two other guys, a Hispanic fellow named Ruben and a Jewish kid from New York City named Ben. We talked, and we even occasionally hung out, drinking beer as we discussed business theories, Camus, and girls. No, we didn't form everlasting, lifelong bonds, but we were cool. College work kept us busy, so our occasions to really hang out and become friends were limited due to our schedules.

I fell into a routine early on in my new environment, which contributed to my success as a student. The social atmosphere didn't wreak havoc with my schedules as it did my peers. I'd been to Europe, been intimate with women, and I'd already experienced New Orleans, so I was better prepared than my contemporaries. Freedom was a new concept for most of them, leading them to explore and discover things and experiences which were old-hat for me. I focused on my studies for the most part, with only a few detours along the way.

Octavia and I talked on the phone at least once a week, but for that first semester it was hard for us to see each other. She was at home working on a new book. According to her, it was an arduous process but she was on a deadline, and would not have time to fly down to spend a weekend with me. She encouraged me to date women in my age group, prompting me to think of Alicia, the prostitute who'd been my first sexual partner. Nothing against Alicia, but I didn't want to go back down the professional path again. I felt I had matured to the point where my interactions with women might be much different than they had been in my past. Octavia was a smart, beautiful bombshell, and I'd managed to form a relationship with her. I wasn't scared or nervous to interact with the females on campus.

Apparently being intimately involved with Octavia more than prepared me to be witty, charming, and dangerous when it came to the young women in my age group. Tulane wasn't the only college campus in greater New Orleans, and without really trying, I was able to enjoy female company whenever I desired. Unlike my male counterparts, I was armed with a weapon none of them knew about or were ready to use—truth. I knew there was no reason to cajole or lie or create a believable story, when I could tell the truth to different women and receive the desired effect.

The secret reality of telling the truth is in doing so, the listener has the choice to do whatever they'd like, without any falsehoods or promises on my part. I'd make and maintain eye contact with a young woman, and we'd strike up a conversation. At some point, either I or my new friend would inquire about the other's availability for a cup of coffee, a drink, dinner, or something more immediate. I always stated I wasn't interested in pursuing a lasting romance, nor was I interested in anything more than having fun, however brief our romantic encounter. Women appreciated my honesty at first, and we engaged in delicious sexual adventures with no strings attached. Of course, some of them later wanted to pursue more time with me, but I stuck to my truth, no matter how alluring or inviting my partner was. It was at that point that I'd cordially distance myself from them, as I'd told them I would in the initial conversation. I didn't lead anyone on, because I didn't want to tread on anyone's feelings. I remained because I wasn't looking for a relationship or a bond, just occasional sex. Callous of me, I know, but I was focused on other things.

I didn't dive into the rest of the social atmosphere of college as I should have. I was too busy studying, too busy planning for my future to get caught up in the sports activities or the parties. Everything I did was geared toward my life after college. In our weekly conversations with Octavia, I would discuss my tentative plans and she would give advice if asked. I planned to take at least two classes each summer, in an effort to eliminate at least one year of my college career. I knew I'd be coming into even more money when I'd turn eighteen, and I planned to use it to start trading stocks, and investing in different companies. As I explained to Octavia, I wanted my inheritance to make more money, aside from the tuition Bobby Jr. had deposited into my account prior to Tulane. I told Octavia of my dream to be a multi-millionaire by the age of twenty-five, with a financial foundation which would allow me to do whatever I liked.

Octavia was as busy as I was. Her romance novels and heroines had garnered such a large following—she was constantly busy with book tours and signings. She'd been back and forth to Hollywood, where she was negotiating a deal to make one of her book series into a movie franchise. Her creative and commercial success might have been overwhelming for someone else, but she seemed to take it in stride.

She never mentioned anything about her son Lars to me, not his progress or achievements, because she knew how I felt about him. Her "in-name-only" marriage to Lawrence was still intact, as they had both agreed the cost of a divorce would be too much of a headache. With our schedules being as busy as they were, we weren't able to see each other until spring break of my freshman year, seven months after our European vacation.

Octavia flew in and booked a suite at a downtown hotel, within a short walking distance of the Quarter. I met her there and we hugged for at least five minutes, basking in each other's presence. I buried my face in her luxuriant red hair, becoming intoxicated by the scent of her, the feel of her in my arms. My Octavia, my lover and best friend.

Even though it wasn't her first time in New Orleans, it was her first time there with me. I was thrilled to be her guide for the week as it would give me the chance to show her the places I loved, as well as taking her to other places she'd never been. It felt similar to how she had shown me the memorable sights of Europe. We spent enjoyable moments biting the heads off of fresh steamed crawfish down at the docks, then dancing till all hours of the morning on Frenchman Street, and making love to each other as if there were no tomorrow, until the sunrise signaled a new day.

If there were truly such a thing as soulmates, Octavia would without a doubt have been mine. She played multiple roles in my life, being both teacher and student, lover and friend, confidante and critic, and mother and sister. Yet due to the circumstances of our age difference and her marriage, we would never have the chance to explore all of the possibilities soulmates could together.

On her last night in New Orleans, we drank wine from dinnertime on in a quiet bar on the outskirts of the Treme. Music drifted in from the neighboring bars but we were in our own bubble, insulated from the world, lost in each other.

"I think you and I are going to be Pen Pals for a while," Octavia said. "You'll be busy exploring and discovering the world which awaits you. I'll be writing and traveling, trying to fulfill my own dreams. We'll try to fit each other into our busy lives, but it'll be difficult."

"Where there's a will, there's always a way," I replied. "If we both make the time and effort to spend time together, we will be fine."

I listened to the words as they came out of my mouth, and I knew I was lying to myself. My heart ached at the truth of her words, and I knew in my soul she was right. I wouldn't want either of us to feel beholden to keeping appointments, in order to appease the selfishness which love demands. We'd be friends and Pen Pals as our own lives moved forward. Maybe we'd somehow manage to be occasional lovers, but I could see such a thing being a rare occurrence.

In her suite later on in the evening, we made love slowly and tenderly, sipping each other like fine wine, savoring the taste, knowing it would be a long time before we saw each other again. I fell asleep with my face in her magnificent hair, our heartbeats in perfect sync.

I left her early the next morning after kissing her on the forehead while she slept, beautiful in repose, resembling a work of art by a Renaissance painter. I'd hold the image of her sleeping in my mind and heart until we met again.

# 16

## 11:59:30

When the wheels have been set in motion, sometimes all a person can do is hold on for the ride. No matter how well one plans, the other shoe always drops, knocking those plans askew. If we knew what the repercussions for our actions would be, we might never attempt them, too horrified at what was wrought because of our hopes and dreams. If only we had time machines, we'd always know the outcome before making a decision.

I enrolled in three classes the summer after my freshman year. Due to the fact I was on scholarship, I had to pay for them myself. No problem. I was determined and focused, ready to get my life started. I aced my classes, adding more credits to my pursuit of a college degree in Business, while at the same time enjoying brief flings with women of all ages and cultures.

I turned eighteen later that summer, and I came into the inheritance from my mother and grandmother. Miss Lenora sent me all of the documentation, including deeds, titles, and account information. From rents paid on the two properties, plus whatever insurance money remained, I was given $68,000. I put $40,000 of it away, and with the rest I started an investment account.

The typical college student knows more about upcoming trends than anyone not working in the investment industry. If someone researched some of the biggest trends over the first years of the new millennium such as social media, technology, fashion, or new music, college students knew about them first, before the rest of the world caught on. The difference between the typical student and me was I had the money to gamble on a few of the new trends. I started cautiously, having studied bulls, bears, upward trends, and anything else associated with the stock market. I was ready. Between playing the stock market and my studies, I left myself little time to play around with my peers.

The routine of my life for the next two years was heady and furiously busy. I became a fanatic about money and an enemy of wasted time. Either I was earning money or learning myriad of ways how to make more of it. Going into my sophomore year I found an apartment not too far away from campus, where I wouldn't have to deal with roommates, noisy freshmen, or anyone else. I loved

119

it, but I knew at some point I would want something more permanent. New Orleans had become home to me and I had no plans to move anywhere else after college, or in the foreseeable future.

Ms. Lenora still managed some of my business as far as making sure I received my checks from my properties. Everything between us was done through the mail and electronic mail. So, I was a bit surprised to receive an email from her requesting a face-to-face meeting with me. Ms. Lenora's message stated she'd be in New Orleans for a weekend in December and she needed to have a conversation with me. We hadn't talked on the phone in two years, so I sent my reply via email. I felt a bit of trepidation about a meeting with her, but I was curious enough to assent. We set an agreed upon time and place, and I anxiously waited for our meeting.

There are many iconic locations in New Orleans, some favored by tourists, others by locals. The restaurant Ms. Lenora had chosen was one of the iconic ones, where the name of the restaurant is actually better than the food they serve. The locals (which I now considered myself) always know a better restaurant, a hipper night club, and the best night on which to attend certain bars.

I was early for my meeting with Ms. Lenora. The outside temperature was hovering around forty degrees, which is cold for New Orleans. People stay indoors as much as they can when the temps dip below fifty. The restaurant only had a few patrons seated at the scattered tables. I sat perusing the menu, while drinking chicory coffee. While trying to decide what to eat, I heard slow footsteps approaching the table. I looked up, surprised and curious.

I recognized her instantly, and I stood up to greet her. I reached to shake her hand and her hazel eyes twinkled merrily. She batted my hand aside and hugged me warmly, as if I were a relative or a friend.

After she finished hugging me, I pulled her chair out for her before returning to my own seat. Words couldn't be found in my brain, and I was speechless.

"Everyone should have at least one person to cheer them on," Ms. Lenora began. "I took it upon myself to show up at your graduation, out of curiosity and pride. You deserved to have someone there, so I came."

Really? I didn't expect anything from anyone, which is why I was so flabbergasted. Bobby Jr. had never shown any interest in me at all, no matter what so-called achievements I'd made. Yet, his secretary had shown up to my graduation, which endeared her to me more than words could ever express.

Ms. Lenora ordered a vodka gimlet from the bored waiter, who'd been hovering near my table since he didn't have many other customers. I ordered an iced lemonade for myself since I wasn't yet in the mood for alcoholic beverages. Our drinks arrived promptly, and Ms. Lenora tapped her glass against mine in a silent toast.

She asked me questions about my studies and my plans for the future. I answered succinctly, having nothing to hide. She nodded her head in approval as I talked of working in the world of finance when college was over. She smiled in appreciation as I told her I would be through with my degree the summer I turned twenty. I had one question burning in my brain, and as she ordered another drink, I took advantage of the pause to ask my question.

"What made you contact me for a meeting?" I asked.

She held up a finger in a gesture for me to wait a minute. Our waiter returned with her second drink, and once he retreated to his perch, Ms. Lenora began to talk.

"I'm forty-seven years old, and I've worked for Bobby for almost twenty years as his secretary and personal assistant. Yet I had no idea of your existence until he requested me to pay the tuition for Boniface," she said. "Curious, I investigated who you were and what your relationship to him was. I learned of your mother's death, plus the financial legacy she'd left you. He put me in charge of collecting the monies from the properties, and made me responsible for your accounts. By your second year at Boniface, Jasper and I decided we would look out for you as much as we could, without Bobby's knowledge."

"Why?" I asked. "Neither of you knew me, and I wasn't your responsibility."

"Jasper said he owed it to your mother's memory," Ms. Lenora said. "Jasper told me the story about a young Black girl who went to work for the Fitzgerald family in an effort to make money for college. Jasper told me Flora Jean was smart, witty, and lively, and wanted to be a nurse. Her relationship with Bobby was a mutual thing, not rape or anything like that. They fell in love with each other as young people tend to do, and everything was secretly peachy for them, as long as no one knew."

"What happened?" I asked, even though I somehow knew the answer.

"Flora Jean became pregnant, and your grandmother Lily went to Mr. and Mrs. Fitzgerald with the notion Bobby and Flora Jean could get married," Ms. Lenora said. "Mr. Fitzgerald shot the idea down, knowing how it would affect his blueprint for Bobby. Mr. Fitzgerald had planned for Bobby to finish school, go to law school, then enter the political arena with the goal of being the governor, or a congressman. A Black wife and a mixed-race family would have buried the dreams of Mr. Fitzgerald. Your grandmother and Mr. Fitzgerald came to an agreement, where Flora Jean would marry Raymond, the handyman, and Bobby would leave town to pursue his education and career elsewhere. Money exchanged hands, papers were signed, and the situation was handled according to the wishes of the parents."

"My mother and Bobby Jr. just went along with it, no problem?" I asked. "If they were so in love, why did they meekly play along? My life would have been very different if they'd fought for each other."

"Mr. Fitzgerald controlled the money, and with the kind of money they have, Bobby really didn't have much of a choice," Ms. Lenora said. "He went to college, and law school, but he refused to go into politics, choosing to make money instead. He rebelled in his own way."

"What about my mother?" I asked, trying to equate the Flora Jean I'd known and loved with the love story I'd just heard.

"Flora Jean and Lily got the properties for which you are the sole owner. According to Jasper she changed afterward, no longer lively, but still smart. She got her degree but she chose to keep working for the family, serving as a daily reminder of the pain they'd wrought."

"Why are you telling me this now?" I asked. "What purpose will it serve?"

"Well, Jasper died a month ago, and he made me promise to tell you about the past in order to prepare you for the future," Ms. Lenora said.

Ms. Lenora waved at the nearby waiter, ordering another drink. She looked at me, smiled, then took it upon herself to order me a whiskey, neat. I ordered a bowl of gumbo plus French bread, needing sustenance all of a sudden. I felt as if her outpouring of stories would require me to have something in my stomach to stop any queasy feelings.

The drinks arrived and Ms. Lenora gestured for me to drink up. I swallowed my whiskey, and felt it burning all the way down to my stomach. The first one always does.

"Jasper thought he would get the chance to help bring you up after Flora Jean's death, but you decided you didn't want to ever return to Mississippi and Bobby was insistent on you going to Boniface," she said. "So, we picked a few places for you to vacation at, with me making all of the arrangements. The chess camp, the bed and breakfast, and the ranch, we considered them to be safe havens. But with some of your other trips, Jasper was worried about you. He arranged to take his vacations at the same time as you, and to the same places. Everywhere you went where I'd pre-arranged your trip, Jasper or I were always there. New Orleans, Chicago, Boston, New York, we made sure you were all right. Europe was actually the first time you were truly alone without either of us being nearby."

Ms. Lenora was smiling now, as my system digested the importance of her words. I'd never been on my own, ever. Even while in Europe, I was with Octavia. I was stunned.

"What about Bobby Jr?" I asked. "What did he think?"

"He only cared about you getting top grades and winning at chess," Ms. Lenora said. "As far as anything else, he really didn't care. He'd read your progress reports and personal letters from your dean, then he'd keep his thoughts to himself, as all good chess players do."

I blinked at her words. Chess player?

"Yes, chess player. Genetics are amazing in every aspect, if a person really thinks about it," she said. "Old Mr. Fitzgerald was a decent chess player and tactician, but he was a ruthless businessman. He used his considerable acumen to maneuver Bobby whenever and however he wanted. Bobby learned how to play the game from Jasper, but he learned to love it on his own. Bobby didn't figure out how well he'd been managed until he was married to a woman his father approved of. It wasn't really a love match. That's when he dropped the bombshell about never entering the political arena. They fought but Bobby won. He decided he'd only follow what he wanted to do. He divorced his wife because he didn't want to be married anymore, and when Mr. Fitzgerald died, he was free to pursue his own dreams."

"My mother?" I asked.

She nodded in assent. "But it didn't work out for them, and he's been cold toward everyone since Flora Jean passed. Apples don't roll too far from the tree, though."

"Meaning what?" I asked, clueless as to where she

was going.

"You're eighteen years old, with over $300,000 in the bank. I don't know how much you have in the secret account you set up, but I'm sure Bobby knows. You speak at least four languages, are a certified wizard in chess, and you grasp most financial nuances effortlessly. In short, you are a prize, just as Bobby was to his father. At some point in the next year and a half he will recruit you, or entreat you to enter his business. In order to control your future, he'll show you the money. And you'll be under his thumb, where he wants you."

"How do you know?" I asked. "I know he didn't share his intentions with you. Chess players don't do that."

"I know the way he thinks, and I have been with him long enough to read his mind. I'm retiring in two or three years, but I want you to be okay for the rest of your life. Whether you decide to work for him or not, never put all of your eggs in his basket. He's cold and calculating, Machiavellian in his schemes. When I retire he'll have a replacement for me, but you won't. I'd like to suggest someone to you when the time comes, someone you can trust as an ally and confidante."

"Who?" My mind was whirling with all of the information I'd been given, my gumbo growing cold on the table in front of us.

Ms. Lenora gestured to the waiter for the check. She rose from the table and I rose with her. She hugged me, and I hugged her in return, trying to show my gratitude for all she'd done on my behalf.

"Make sure to keep me in the loop, and when the time is right my daughter, Dolores, will begin working with you," she said after our hug. "Be ready for her, and prepare for your father to make his first move."

Ms. Lenora exited the restaurant, leaving me alone with my thoughts and the check.

# 17

# 11:59:31

The best way to win any game, from chess to badminton, is to be mentally prepared. Study, practice, whatever is required. The problems in life occur when we're blindsided by the unexpected. The unexpected is what wins or loses the game, no matter what the game may be.

I remained steadfast in my education, studying business models, and readying myself for the future. Of course, I shared the information I'd learned from Ms. Lenora with Octavia. Her advice was to be vigilant in the pursuit of my own dreams, never mind what anyone else had planned for my life. As usual I did my best to heed her advice, because her words always came from the heart.

For my spring break I vacationed with Octavia in Key West, for which she had made all the arrangements. Octavia had rented a private beach house where we could relax, laugh, and cook for ourselves if we wanted to. Every evening Octavia and I would join hands, and walk down to the water to watch the sunset with the other gathered tourists and locals. It was an amazing sight, watching the golden sunsets from the southernmost point in America.

We ventured out every day, and not just for the sunsets. We ate at local restaurants, sipped beers and margaritas in the bars and cantinas, and we spent a lovely afternoon touring the house of Ernest Hemingway. I wasn't a big fan of his, even though I read most of his works. Octavia was, which explained her need to see where he lived. I teased her, telling how one day, fifty years in the future, a fan of hers would want to visit where she had lived and worked. I thought she would laugh, but she rose and kissed me on the cheek.

"Thank you," she whispered.

Of course, we also spent plenty of the week blissfully enjoying each other's company. We shared deep and intimate conversations, along with intense and tender lovemaking, during which there were mutual whispered promises to attempt to see each other as much as our schedules permitted. At the end of the week we ferried to Miami, then hugged farewell at the airport.

I took summer classes again, eliminating all of my electives, meaning I might be able to eliminate my senior year. I earned another forty grand over the summer with my investments, and I was sitting pretty when I returned to school in the fall. I'd routinely check in with Ms. Lenora, except our conversations were much more personal. It was a welcome change.

The year just seemed to speed by. Octavia and I might miss a week or two without talking, because I had taken five classes in my effort to be completed with college by May. My social life was a daydream, because I didn't have time for one in any capacity. For some reason I felt like there was a clock was ticking down, and I had to beat it.

I rested in my apartment for the holidays, enjoying drinking beer and relaxing. I talked to Octavia often during the holidays, attempting to entice her into coming to visit, just for a couple of days. She claimed she was too busy and unable to get away right then. I shrugged it off, understanding how elusive time is. I told Octavia I'd begun looking at houses in the French Quarter, Metairie, and the Garden District. I planned on purchasing a house of my own when I graduated in May. She asked what my requirements in a house were and I told her I didn't have many. I promised to keep her posted as to what my search results yielded.

I wanted a house so I could have a backyard, a garden, and I'd finally buy myself one of the cars I'd often daydreamed of driving. Maybe I'd take a road trip, something I'd never done. I had visions of the open roads of the American West, of mountains and some of the things I'd only ever seen in books. It was a possibility I was looking forward to.

After conferring with school officials, I took five classes again for the second semester. They had confirmed I'd meet the degree requirements with these last five classes. After May, I would be free of school forever, no more tests, and no more wasting time. I saw no need to chase an MBA, because I already had the knowledge and experience I needed for the future. I was ready for the real world—or at least I thought so.

With my nose to the grindstone I plodded on, inching closer to my goal. On the weekends I'd sleep some, then spend the majority of my time looking at houses all over New Orleans. I didn't rule out anywhere, because I know it is sometimes possible to find a diamond in the rough, a masterpiece in disguise.

In February I found one of those disguised masterpieces. The house was in the Garden District, and it seemed to call out to me. There were four bedrooms, two and a half bathrooms, a huge kitchen, plus a carriage house, a huge yard, and a long driveway. The price was rather steep, but luckily it was not beyond my means. I wanted to buy it right then and move in immediately, but I'd promised myself I'd wait until May after graduation. May seemed so far away.

I called Octavia excitedly, telling her about the location, describing the amenities and the price. She seemed excited for me, but she said she was a little bit under the weather, nothing serious. I told her to get better soon, because it was almost time for us to discuss our annual spring break plans.

I was studying frantically, making sure all of my papers were turned in, cramming excessively for final exams. I was pretty smart, but college is not a walk in the park, trust me. I was adhering strictly to my routine, leaving myself time for school, quick meals, and sleep. No movies, newspapers, or television shows. I would catch up on what was happening in the world once I had my degree. One week before spring break, it dawned on me that I hadn't heard from Octavia. It had been a month since we'd talked. On my way to sleep on a Wednesday night, I promised myself I'd call her the next day.

That Thursday, I went through my regular routine of classes, impatient for the college rigmarole to be over. By the time I returned to my apartment that afternoon, I was exhausted mentally and physically. I retrieved my mail from the mailbox and went upstairs to the apartment. I tossed the mail on the counter then collapsed into a deep slumber, worn out from my day.

I woke a few hours later, groggy and hungry. I ordered a pizza, popped open a beer and decided to open my mail. Since I was so young, my mail usually consisted of advertising circulars and utility bills, so the official looking envelope took me by surprise. The return address was a lawyer's office in South Bend, Indiana. Just as I was about to open it my doorbell rang signaling my pizza had arrived. I set the letter back down and paid for my pizza. I forgot about the letter as I dined on pizza and drank a beer.

As I was cleaning up, preparing to go to bed, I remembered the envelope. I grabbed it and finished opening it.

*"Dear Mr. Jackson,*
*Our client and friend, Mrs. Octavia Patricia Sullivan*

*Nicholls, passed away early last week. As her executors, your presence is requested in our office, Tuesday, March 16th as you are mentioned in her last will and testament. If you are unable to attend, please notify us in advance. If you need help of any kind, we are at your service."*

I sat down in stunned disbelief. I'd talked to her only a month before, and she had not made her illness sound very serious at all. I was shocked, hurt, bewildered, and lost. Unwanted visions of my mother lying in a pool of blood came unwanted into my brain. I questioned God as to why everyone I'd ever loved died before their time. My tears were of no solace as I wept with no control, and my mind was alive with the memories of Octavia.

In my grief-stricken state I automatically dialed the number of the one person who had always comforted me, but the phone just rang and rang. It took Octavia's voice on her answering service to bring it home—she would never answer my phone calls again. I hung up the phone and sat there on the floor, destroyed and bereft.

# 18

## 11:59:32

To this day, I can still smell my grandmother Lily's Juicy Fruit chewing gum. If I close my eyes, I can still hear my mother Flora Jean's musical laughter and her beautiful singing voice. I can't look at the color red without thinking of how good it felt to run my fingers through Octavia's luxuriant hair. Grieving doesn't ever end, no matter what anyone has read, seen, or been told. I would be strolling along, whistling happily, just as carefree as imaginable. A woman's laugh could come floating on the air out of a café, and it would remind me so much of my mother I'd immediately sink into a state of depression. We never fully heal from grief, and time is only a temporary balm.

I had to make flight reservations which normally would have irked me, but it kept my brain occupied. Normally Ms. Lenora would have handled all of my arrangements, but this situation felt as if I needed to handle it myself. I scoured the newspapers from the previous week, and I found her death notice in the obituary section of the Picayune. Her books were listed as well as a movie based on one of her books. Her birth and death were listed, the cause of death being referred to as a long illness. The article listed her surviving husband and son, but that was it. I didn't know what long illness she'd suffered from, but maybe I'd find out more when I attended the reading of the will.

I landed at the small regional airport, and caught a taxi to my hotel. Sleep was an elusive stranger as it had been every night since I'd gotten the death notification. I couldn't sleep, thinking of our many adventures and shared intimacies. I needed to get to the lawyer's office early, to find out what long illness had taken away my beloved.

I dressed carefully the next morning, making sure my tie was knotted correctly and my shoes were shined to a high gloss. I knew of at least one person who wouldn't be happy to see me. Well, if you think about it, the whole situation was the fault of Lars Jr. Would thanking him be too much of a slap in the face? I'd have to play it by ear.

The office wasn't too far from the small hotel where I was staying, so I walked over with thirty minutes to spare. I wanted to be there first, before any imagined shenanigans could take place. It was a typical upscale lawyer's office, dark wood paneling, inoffensive art on the walls, and a secretary peering at me ominously over her glasses. I greeted her with a good morning, and gave her my full name. She informed her superior over the intercom of my arrival. He opened the door to his inner sanctum and beckoned me in.

He introduced himself and offered his plump, manicured hand for a handshake. I obliged and he showed me to my seat. There were five chairs set up in his office, so I assumed four other people would be attending. As he settled behind his desk, I waited a moment before asking my questions.

"How did she die? What long illness did she pass away from?"

"Mrs. Nicholls had suffered from refractory pulmonary hypertension," the lawyer said. "She suffered with it for years, but it finally wore her down and won. She was a fighter and she made the best of her situation. She managed to flourish while combating an incurable, degenerative disease."

I tried to recall occasions where she'd been overly tired or out of breath, but I couldn't. Even after frenetic lovemaking sessions, she never appeared to have been struggling to breathe. If she had, I simply chalked it up to the physicality of our sexual escapades. She took pills, but I'd never questioned her about them. I had always assumed hypertension was a simple, easily treated disease. I was mistaken.

The intercom buzzed, and the lawyer walked to the door to usher in the other attendees. Lawrence Nicholls Sr. looked at me, then nodded at me as if he knew me. He was a bigger, wider version of his assboil of a son. A slender, bespectacled woman followed him into the room. She smiled at me slightly, then took her seat. Lars was the last person to enter the office. He closed the door behind him, then his eyes met mine.

"What the fuck are you doing here?" he asked. He was glaring at me furiously, his face beginning to turn red. I couldn't help myself. I cracked up laughing for the first time since I'd received the letter. This meeting was going to be epic.

"He has no right to be here!" Lars shouted.

"He has every right to be here, because he's named in her will," Lawrence Nicholls said. "Now sit down and shut up, before I make you wait outside."

Still breathing heavily, the beet-red Lars stalked to a seat and plopped down angrily. His response made me realize just how little his brain was. It seemed there had been no mental growth since I'd last seen him. I was sorry for Octavia in that moment, because he was her son and she had loved him.

The secretary appeared then, handing everyone a glass of water, except for the pitiful Lars. I thanked her, because I really needed it. I don't know how she knew I was thirsty or if it was just protocol. Nervously, I sipped my water as the lawyer began to read Octavia's last will and testament aloud. I put my head down and listened.

To summarize, Octavia left the bulk of her estate and assets to her only son, Lawrence Nicholls Jr. Which was only right, as he was her only child. Her husband wasn't mentioned at all, but he was rich in his own right. Various charities received bequests, and then it got down to the nitty-gritty and the reason for my presence.

"To my secretary and confidante, Melanie Perkins, I leave two million dollars, and the media rights to all of my novels," the lawyer read. I met the eyes of the bespectacled woman, who I surmised was Melanie, because tears were rolling down her face. I was happy for her, but I wondered just how much Melanie knew about me. My name being spoken by the lawyer startled me out of my reverie.

"His friendship and love could never be repaid, and I leave him the title to a house I purchased for him as a graduation gift, and 300,000 dollars so he will never be beholden to anyone and free to pursue his dreams."

I was stunned, flabbergasted, and my grief was threatening to overwhelm me. Lars rescued me by displaying himself as the biggest asshole in the room.

"I'm contesting this will!" he shouted. "What right does this nigger have to anything of my mother's? I will not stand—" Smack. His words were cut off by a firm slap in the mouth from his father.

"Do not embarrass her any further. Go wait in the car, or I'll contest your portion of her estate," Lawrence said. He was so calm and collected, admirable even.

The red-faced Lars hurriedly left the room, his hand still on his cheek where his father had slapped him.

"That's everything," the lawyer said. "Ms. Perkins and Mr. Jackson, if you'll kindly step to my secretary's desk and sign the paperwork, you can be on your way."

The lawyer held the door open for Ms. Perkins to leave, but a look from Lawrence Nicholls caused the lawyer to exit after Ms. Perkins, closing the door behind him. I was alone with Octavia's husband.

"Octavia earned every dollar she made on her own," he said. "With that being said, my son will not contest her decisions regarding the allocation of her money. I apologize for my son's behavior today, and his behavior to you in the past. As for your relationship with my wife, I'd like to thank you for being who you were to her."

He extended his hand to me, shocking the shit out of me. I returned the gesture and shook hands with him.

"Our marriage was different than most," he said. "Over the last months of her life as her illness got worse, we exchanged confidences, and in doing so, we became the best of friends. Octavia told me your story and of the part you and she played in each other's lives. My son is my cross to bear because the way he turned out is my fault. I owe it to his mother to do my best to redirect the course of his life as best I can. I offered to call you during her last days, but she wouldn't let me because you needed to concentrate on your studies. Enjoy everything you've been given today, Mr. Jackson. Octavia would want you to live life to the fullest, as she did. If you have any problems with my son or anything else, here's my card. I'll be available if you need me."

Lawrence handed me his business card, then we shook hands again, and he departed. I was alone, again, literally and spiritually.

I signed the required paperwork, receiving a certified check and the keys to my new house. I shook hands with the lawyer and made my exit. When I stepped out into the sunlight, Ms. Perkins was waiting on the sidewalk. She was smiling at me and her head was tilted to the side, appraising me.

"Would you like to have lunch with me, Mr. Jackson?" she asked. "My afternoon is free and I'm not leaving for California until tomorrow."

Always look for the silver lining in every situation in life. Always.

# 19

## 11:59:33

W hen one door closes, another door opens. Yet what if we are scared or unwilling to open a new door? What if the past represented by the closed door prohibits us from new opportunities? Scars and wounds don't heal overnight, leaving us fragile and unsure as to what comes next.

My lunch with Octavia's assistant, Melanie, was both light and informative. She'd been Octavia's secretary for seven years, yet she was only twenty-eight. Through our lunch, as we munched on sandwiches and chips, she shared everything she knew about my relationship with Octavia. Melanie had made the Europe arrangements. She picked up a small satchel she'd been carrying, and handed it across the table to me.

I unzipped the leather satchel and withdrew a photo album. Opening it up, the first picture was of a younger me, posing in the Poet's Corner of Westminster Abbey. I remembered her taking the picture because photographs were frowned upon in Westminster Abbey. Flipping through the album there were pictures of Octavia and me over the years, in many different locales. With tears rolling down my face, I looked up at Melanie and said, "Thank you, you have no idea what this means to me."

"Now, we should toast Octavia in a way she'd have approved of," Melanie said. "Let's find a liquor store and we can return to the hotel, where we can drink privately."

My libido stirred, as I looked at Melanie appraisingly. She was slim, yet curvy, and her glasses added an underlying sexiness. I nodded my head in agreement, and we paid our bill prior to departing on this spontaneous adventure.

We perused the local liquor store's offerings before agreeing upon a bottle of red wine, Guinness, and a fifth of Irish whiskey. I watched Melanie's skirt twitching enchantingly as she went to pay for our liquor. I wasn't in New Orleans, and I was still underage according to my driver's license.

We walked companionably toward the hotel, flirting a little, and in doing so, bolstering each other's spirits. I carried the satchel containing the photo album, which I'd also put my check and house keys into. Melanie cheerfully carried the alcohol, saying since she was the only legal adult, she'd carry it.

Standing in front of the hotel, leaning on a pillar, as if he'd been waiting for us, Lars stood at attention as we approached. I quietly handed Melanie the satchel, unsure of what he would do, but confident in what my response would be.

"I should have known," he said. "A gold digger and a sneaky nigger, in cahoots with each other. Celebrating how you scammed my mother, huh? I refuse to let you enjoy her money."

He approached us aggressively, and I sent a silent prayer upward to Octavia, asking for forgiveness.

"Your mother was the smartest, nicest woman I've ever had the pleasure of making love to," I said. "If it wasn't for you being such a racist asshole, I'd have never had the privilege."

Lars swung at me then, and I slid sideways to avoid his punch. I quickly and effectively counterpunched, left, right, left, right, stunning him. I moved in, avoiding his weak, ineffective attempts, and I beat his ass right there, in front of Melanie and the hotel patrons who'd come out to see the hullabaloo. I hit him for all of the racial slurs I'd endured, all of the loneliness I had experienced at Boniface, and for his mother, who would have been ashamed of him. I caught him with a right uppercut to the chin, which not only ended the fight, but knocked him out cold.

As I stood over him, fists clinched, I couldn't help myself. Blood poured copiously from his nose and mouth, and I said to him in his unconscious state, "Checkmate."

As the hotel security tried to figure out what to do, I calmly used Melanie's cell phone to call the number on the business card I'd received earlier. Two policemen jumped out of their cruiser, siren wailing, and ran toward me, hands on their batons. Silently, I handed the phone to the first officer as he got close. He took the phone from me and listened to the voice on the other end. Shaking his head, he handed the phone back to me. Gesturing to his partner to sheathe his baton, they lifted Lars off of the ground and put him in the back of the police car. They turned the siren off and drove away.

I thanked Mr. Lawrence Nicholls for his help, assuring him I was all right. I hung up the phone, still tripping out on how crazy life can be. Melanie accompanied me to my room. She ordered two buckets of ice from room service, and when they arrived, she soaked my fists in ice, while she prepared drinks. Pouring whiskey on the rocks into glasses for both of us, she raised hers to me in a toast. I lifted mine in return.

"To Octavia," she said. We clinked our glasses together, and the fiery Irish whiskey burned its way down my throat. Melanie found a smooth jazz station on the radio, and the wailing horns and soothing bass lines served as a soundtrack for our evening. By the third drink, the heat of the whiskey no longer burned my mouth. In fact, another kind of heat was pervading the atmosphere of my hotel room. By the fifth drink Melanie was astride me, her glasses and skirt both having been discarded. I was buried in her, letting her furiously ride me towards my climax. I exploded inside of her as she threw back her head and screamed out her own climax. I sat there, listening to our rhythmic breathing, knowing we still had alcohol and time. It was the best memorial I'd ever been involved in. We shared a memorable night, bolstered by whiskey, music, and lovemaking.

Thanks for everything, Octavia. Rest in peace. I think I'll be okay going forward.

# 20

## 11:59:35

In chess, as in life, the best offense is often a good defense. When planning, it's best to think the way an enemy or opponent would—that way, they can be defeated using their own strategy. A smart person will try to pinpoint their own weakness, in order to thwart their enemy's attempts. Always try to be prepared for the worst, but hope for the best.

It wasn't easy for me to refocus on my studies when I returned to New Orleans. I kept myself going by daydreaming about life after I got my degree. I had the house of my dreams, and I was slowly moving my things in. I walked through it, imagining where I would hang paintings and place the furniture. It wouldn't be furnished fully overnight, but I had plenty of time with which to make my visions a reality. I'd started sending my resume out to companies in and around New Orleans. If I didn't get any offers I liked, I'd rent office space and start my own company. I possessed little fear at all. I was confident about my future success.

Melanie had promised to keep in touch, and I told her if I ever got out to California, I'd look her up. She'd be busy herself, trying to get Octavia's books turned into movies. I told her to keep me in mind if she ever got a hankering for gumbo and good music. It couldn't hurt to have another person with a good opinion of me. Our night had been a one-time thing, with the possibility of future meetings.

I chose not to participate in the graduation ceremony. I didn't have any family or anything, so it wasn't a big deal to me. Ms. Lenora had asked me, but I told her there was no need for her to come down. She said I should be on the lookout for her graduation presents. My curiosity was piqued, but she wouldn't tell me what she'd gotten me.

Bobby Jr. sent me a telegram, not a letter, requesting my presence for a lunch meeting. He would be in town for a few days and he wanted to see me. The telegram sounded more like a command than a request, but I'd go out of curiosity. Ms. Lenora's warning to me had me both wary and intrigued about the meeting.

In May I received my Bachelors Degree in Business from Tulane University. They mailed it to me and I framed it so I could hang it in my home office. My new house was sparsely furnished, but my office had a desk, fax machine, printer, and a computer. I'd be equipped to work at home, whether I found a job or not. I'd gotten a couple of inquiries from companies, but they hadn't set up any interviews with me. I'd see what developed, but I was not in a hurry.

I dressed casually for our lunch meeting, to show him it wasn't a big deal to me. I hadn't seen him in years, and I was no longer a little boy, trying to garner some kind of affection from him. It was too late for any of that. Maybe we'd have some kind of relationship but I doubted if there'd ever be a familial connection.

Bobby Jr. was seated at a back table when I arrived. He stood to shake my hand, but he had to incline his head upward. I stood six-foot-three, and he was maybe five-foot-eleven. I admit, I felt a little surge of assurance based on being taller than him. Yes, I know it was a petty thought to have on my part.

"You've certainly grown up," he said as we sat down. "Let's order some drinks and appetizers, and you can catch me up on your plans."

Bobby Jr. confidently ordered two beers and two whiskeys, followed by a plate of fried shrimp and charbroiled oysters. I wasn't a fan of oysters, but I'd definitely eat the shrimp. This was surreal, something I'd daydreamed about a few times in my life—having drinks with my father.

"So now you've gotten your degree, what's next?" he asked. "Tell me your plans, if you don't mind." Maybe he felt entitled, due to the financial role he had played in my life. Or maybe he was just moving his queen into attack position. No matter.

"I've sent my resume to a few brokerage firms, hoping for an entry level position," I said. "I think I'll start my own investment firm at some point, but I'll build up my credentials working for someone else."

He drank his beer down in one gulp, then chased it with oysters. I sipped my drink, waiting for his response. I'd moved my pawn two spaces forward, readying myself to play defense. Bobby Jr. didn't disappoint.

"An entry level position at a brokerage might start you out at about 40,000 dollars a year, plus commissions, maybe," he said. "How would you feel about accepting, shall we say, an apprenticeship with Fitzgerald Industries? Before you respond, let me give you an overview. My company is invested in logistics, lumber, finance, and just about anything you could think of which makes money. I know you're qualified because I know your talents. The first year you'll make at least $100,000, plus bonuses and commissions on any new business you put us into. By the time you're finished with your apprenticeship, the CFO position will be waiting for you."

I was stunned. Bobby Jr. had laid out an offer much better than anything I could have imagined. The money sounded good, but the potential outweighed the money. I'd be set for life, plus I'd be doing something I was interested in. Maybe I hesitated a bit too long, because he plunged right back in.

"There'll be plenty of travel, which I know is one of your interests," he said. "You can still be based in New Orleans, especially with the whole Internet thing keeping you constantly connected. I'll guide you personally and from afar, but I will take charge of your apprenticeship.

Just give me the word, and I'll have a contract sent to you Monday."

"I'm going to need a few days to think your offer over," I said. The enormity of my decision was the only reason I requested more time. Honestly, I was ready to accept then, but I wanted to research his company thoroughly as I would any other company.

"No problem. Take your time, but I need to know by next Friday. I'll need to alter my schedule in order to get you started. Are you sure you don't want any of these oysters?"

I shook my head. Smoothly, as we drank our beers, he steered the conversation into sports, Internet related business, and politics. The offer wasn't mentioned again, which I appreciated. We drank a couple of more beers companionably, then Bobby glanced at his watch.

"Well, I've enjoyed this lunch, but I have other fish to fry while I'm here," he said. "You have all of my numbers, so contact me with your answer. I'll pick up the tab for this meal, no problem."

Bobby Jr. stood up, as did I, and we shook hands. As I was getting ready to leave, a thought occurred to me.

"What should I call you?" I asked.

"Just call me Bobby, okay? And I'll call you Jackson." He sat back down before saying, "Let's keep it simple."

I left the restaurant, his offer heavy on my mind. It was a sultry, steamy day in New Orleans, when all a person can want to do is peel off their skin and lay down in a pool of cool water. I idly began to think about the possibility of having a pool built at my new house. I could definitely afford it, but would I have the time? As I walked along, on my way to my house, I figured it was finally time for me to go and buy a car. Different models ran through my brain, and as I started the walk up my driveway, I'd narrowed my choices to three or four different cars.

I pulled up suddenly, because the landscape of my front porch had changed. There was a porch swing on it with a ribbon attached to it. Sitting on the swing was the prettiest, most chocolate woman I'd ever seen, in person or on television. Stunned speechless, I could only look into her beautiful hazel eyes.

"I'm Dolores, your graduation gift," she said, then giggled. "The look on your face is priceless. My mama sent me to be your personal assistant and secretary. She wanted it to be a surprise."

I started smiling then, thankful for Ms. Lenora. I'd make sure to call her and thank her personally. Dolores had a linen business suit on, which did not detract from the feminine curves which couldn't be hidden. I made a vow to myself to keep our relationship as businesslike as possible.

"Wanna go buy a car with me?" I asked.

# 21

# 11:59:36

The most personal question we can ask ourselves is this—am I a team player? Everyone's automatic response is to tell themselves yes, when in reality they probably aren't. We all like to think we'd willingly sacrifice for the good of the team, but it's a lie. The "What about me?" factor dooms partnerships, relationships, franchises, teams, and possibilities, because none of us are that unselfish.

I called a cab for Dolores and me. I was serious about buying a new car, plus I wanted to learn what talents she brought to the table. I knew Ms. Lenora's capabilities, but I wasn't sure of her daughter's skill level.

As we sat on the porch waiting, Dolores told me about herself. In a nutshell, she was Ms. Lenora's oldest child and only daughter. She'd worked every summer alongside her mother, learning how to do pretty much everything. Dolores had just received her college degree from Jackson State the week before.

"I couldn't wait to leave Mississippi and see the world," she said. "Other than a few family trips, I haven't really been anywhere. My mother started grooming me for this job two years ago. She thinks highly of you, and she said you're gonna need me."

I laughed a little bit then, wondering how much Ms. Lenora had told her. As if she'd read my mind, Dolores started talking again.

"I've been in charge of your accounts for a while now, and I have all of the documentation in my briefcase," she said. "My mother made sure I was familiar with everything about you, and I am. Your family history, plus your educational history. Whatever other secrets you possess, I'll learn them eventually."

I was slightly amused by her certainty, but I believed her. Dolores was her mother's daughter, and I'd never doubt her veracity. I'd do my best to keep our relationship as businesslike as possible, even though I felt an undeniable attraction between us.

In the taxi I pointed out the sights of New Orleans to Dolores, telling her bawdy tales of the city's history and my own personal stories of drunkenness which had her laughing aloud. I promised her she'd get to experience New Awlins once she got settled in, which made me ask her about her accommodations.

"I have a one-bedroom apartment downtown which I signed a one-year lease for," she said. "After a year, I'll decide if I want to stay here or not. Which reminds me, my mother has been paying me what you'd been paying her, but I need a considerable raise. Especially since I don't know what our business will be."

I told Dolores she'd get a substantial raise and I'd have a contract for her in the next couple of days. The taxi stopped and I helped Dolores out after I paid the driver. The car dealership was a first-time experience for me, so I was doubly glad I had her with me. We were escorted around the car lot by an overanxious salesman, and I let Dolores do all of the talking. I cleared my throat while standing next to a Cadillac sedan with a sunroof. She took the hint.

Less than forty-five minutes later, she and I were on I-10 heading east, with me driving my first car, a blue Cadillac sedan, which Dolores had gotten for $10,000 less than the list price. Once she'd explained to the salesmen there would be no need for a finance company, they were willing to do whatever she asked. I observed her in action, and told myself I'd send Ms. Lenora a dozen roses as soon as possible. Dolores was a treasure. I knew from how she'd handled the salesman she'd be an asset to me in my varied business interests.

I pulled off the highway east of the city. Once a person drives east of the city, they're out in the country. I pulled the car into a hole-in-the-wall restaurant with a blinking neon sign which read *Lucky's*. The gravel-covered parking lot was about half-full of old pick-up trucks and a few other cars, none of which were less than three years old. After I helped Dolores out of the car, I opened the trunk and put her briefcase inside of it. Walking towards the door, the air was permeated with the mouthwatering smell of fried food. I pushed the door open to the sound of the blues. I held it for Dolores and I followed behind her to a table, doing my best not to ogle the tantalizing swish of her curvy hips.

We sat at an ancient table, with what seemed like the initials of everyone who lived in the parish carved into it. Lucky's was rich in ambience and our waitress seemed to be part of the decor. She was chewing gum with a rhythm akin to a machine gun, and her aura seemed to be one of no-nonsense. She greeted us, then she ran through the specials of the day.

"Y'all want catfish, chicken, or shrimp? They all come with jambalaya and a slice of bread," our server informed us.

I ordered the catfish, a pitcher of beer, and Dolores ordered the chicken. Our waitress lumbered away, returning with a pitcher of beer and two ice cold glasses. She poured our beer and left. I can still taste the cold crispness of the beer we drank at Lucky's.

"What's the plan?" Dolores asked, wiping foam from her lips.

I quit staring at her lips long enough to say the first words to come to my brain.

"I want to be rich," I said. "I want to have money enough to do whatever I want to do, whenever I want to do it. You with me?"

Dolores raised her glass in a mock toast to my words. "Sounds like a winning plan to me. How are we going to do it?"

Our steaming food arrived then and between bites of tender, flaky catfish, I outlined to Dolores everything Bobby had offered to me.

"I'm going to accept his offer, but I want you to find us some reasonable office space to rent," I said. "I'll learn everything from him, and I'll excel in his company, but you and I will operate our own business, aside from what I do with him. I'm not putting all of my eggs into the basket of Bobby Fitzgerald, because I haven't relied on anything from him to this point."

"I'll get on that in the morning, and I should have some likely prospects by tomorrow evening," she replied. "It shouldn't be hard, and I'll concentrate on getting everything up and running."

As we drank beer and ate our food I looked at Dolores, and was extremely grateful for the graduation gift Ms. Lenora had given me.

# 22

# 11:59:38

Two dance partners who have practiced together, and danced constantly together, look almost flawless in the execution of their movements. Astaire and Rogers come to mind, because no matter what other partners Astaire may have had, Ginger Rogers is the only one who anyone remembers with clarity. Every person does not possess the right moves or instincts to make for the perfect partner.

Dolores made shit happen, which is about as blunt as I can be. Within a week, we had office space in an office building out in Kenner. The rent was fairly cheap, and we signed a one-year lease with the option to renew. I gave her access to the account I'd been using for my investments. We were both dedicated and diligent, even though I was extremely busy with the apprenticeship.

Bobby had me working in an office downtown, which was a small satellite office for Fitzgerald Industries. He showed me how many different entities Fitzgerald Industries was invested in and it was almost as if they were printing money. Anything on which a dollar could be made, Fitzgerald Industries was involved in. Since Bobby had taken over the company, he'd put the company into all sorts of new business. When I had been a little boy, the Fitzgeralds were invested in lumber, paper, and property. Now, they had both domestic and international concerns, employing over 10,000 people around the globe. He'd turned his father's regional juggernaut into a modern, international financial empire.

Dolores was with me every step of the way, whether in person, via email, or on the phone. My new schedule totally killed any ideas I may have had of a social life. I was able to enjoy an evening dinner every now and then with Dolores, but we mostly talked business, striving to not let our relationship become intimate. Not an easy accomplishment when one considers the many ways we were tied together.

Investing on our own, with the insider's knowledge I was learning at my job, had my investment account swelling. It was a powerful feeling to know I'd built enough capital on my own to withstand any downturns in my life, or so I felt. I was still as voracious a learner as I'd ever been, but now I was learning how many ways there were to accumulate money.

When a person is constantly busy, time flies by swiftly. My twenty-first and twenty-second birthdays were soon in the rearview mirror of my life, and my time as an apprentice was coming to an end. Bobby had given me the keys to the kingdom by teaching me the ins and outs of Fitzgerald Industries. I knew the phone numbers of most of the key people in the company, I knew how each division ran, and I figured I knew ways to make each component run better.

I convinced Bobby to let me handle the investment arm of the company, which he agreed to as soon as the question was out of my mouth. I quickly invested the company in solar energy, Internet-driven businesses, and I backed off of some of the other investments which were becoming dinosaurs. Bobby had been mistaken when he'd told me I'd be a millionaire by the age of twenty-five. I was a millionaire at twenty-two.

Now, regarding my personal life, or lack thereof, I dated rarely and had sex even less than that. I was too busy and I did not have the time available to court, woo, or bed any new woman. Dolores and I continued our dance of hands-off, yet she and I flirted shamelessly, as if waiting for the other person to flinch. We were like a bomb with a lit fuse, knowing there'd be a huge explosion at some point in the future.

Bobby kept his word and named me the CFO of Fitzgerald Industries, but then he surprised me by saying I'd have to shut down my side business. He said it might reek of insider trading if I was ever investigated by the FCC. I hadn't thought about the ramifications and I assured him I'd divest myself as soon as possible. He told me we would talk once a week about business, because he had another project which would keep him busy. Bobby never went into details about his projects, keeping his thoughts to himself as any chess player should.

It's funny—we respected each other's acumen as far as business, but the fatherly aspect I'd once had hopes for never materialized. Our conversations never went below the surface of our current relationship. We never discussed Flora Jean or our blood kinship, and I'd learned not to expect it. He was an intensely private man who never discussed his personal life, unless it was with God.

Ms. Lenora had retired, pretty much following the timeline she'd given me. She and her husband, Dolores' father, retired to Arizona, while both were still young enough to find new things to do. Ms. Lenora was her daughter's sounding board for decision making, and her words of wisdom seemed to always help us. But she didn't know what secret project Bobby was working on either, and had no clues to share with me.

I called Dolores and told her to make us reservations at a swanky restaurant where we could drink and eat. I informed her it would be a night of celebration and lamentation, so she should dress for it. No briefcases needed.

I should have picked her up, but I wasn't thinking. Her house was only a few blocks from mine but I'd never been there. I tried desperately to stay on my side of the relationship line. Dolores was my right hand in all of my endeavors and I didn't want to ruin it by crossing the line. She'd sent me a text telling me the time and place. Of course, I beat her there due to my insistence on always being early. I was feeling pretty good about most things, but just a bit sad about having to shut down our side operation.

When she walked in, my breath halted for a moment. Dolores was dressed to the nines, her outfit clinging to the curves God had given her. My mouth was dry as I pulled out her chair for her. Her little black dress was classy, yet sensual. The ripeness of her figure spoke to every male instinct inside of me, making me long for just a single sip of Dolores. I had to be steadfast in my determination not to destroy our partnership.

We ordered drinks, a margarita for her, and a whiskey on the rocks for me. When the waiter asked if we would like to order our food, I told him we wanted to enjoy drinks for a while. With the amount of money I knew I would spend, the restaurant could wait until we were ready. I had grown used to hovering servers and knew it was best to tell them exactly what was required.

"I invited you to dinner so we could celebrate our success, and plan for our future," I said. "Bobby told me I'd have to shut down our side business for fear it may lead to FCC investigations for insider trading. So I figured you and I should discuss how to dismantle our operation and how to split the profits."

"I'm not the new CFO of Fitzgerald Industries, and I don't work for them, so why do I need to stop?" Dolores asked. "Why can't I just buy you out and continue on my own? If we subtract your initial investment and earnings, then split everything else, you can just walk away."

"I hadn't even thought of it. I just assumed you'd be content to continue as my assistant with Fitzgerald," I said. "Are you?"

"No, that's not enough for me. It's my time to fly, and I'm ready," Dolores said.

I ordered another round of drinks, remaining silent until the drinks were served. In all of my planning and plotting, I'd never considered Dolores not being with me. I gulped my drink, panicked by the prospect of not having her with me as an ally or sounding board. Our partnership was successful in everything we'd attempted. Shit.

"What are we going to do?" I asked. Our second round of drinks had arrived, right on time, because I needed another.

Dolores broke down all of our finances, our bank accounts, and the equitable division of our assets. She said she'd continue alone, expanding on what we'd started. She also suggested taking my name off of everything, and I remain involved as a silent partner. The way her mind worked just added to the allure of her. I could take a single check from her buying me out, or I could remove my name and receive quarterly checks. Either way, it was a win for me.

We ordered another round of drinks, then appetizers. Her cleavage seemed to be mocking me, the roundness of her ebony globes mesmerizing. I felt a familiar stirring in my loins, aided by the alcohol and her physical assets. I had an epiphany then, one which brought a smile to my face. She looked at me quizzically.

"If I'm going to receive quarterly checks from you, then I'm only an investor, right?" I asked. "If so, we're no longer partners in any shape or form. Right?"

"Correct. Just business associates," Dolores said.

Her hazel eyes twinkled at me as if she knew what I was getting at. If we weren't business partners, then maybe we could explore other avenues of our relationship. At least in my mind we could. I like to think she was in agreement with my thoughts.

Dinner didn't seem important anymore. We finished our appetizers, and I suggested we go somewhere else to keep celebrating. Dolores smiled at me and nodded in agreement.

"Like we're on a date?" she asked. Then she cracked up laughing. "Let's go have some fun, and make a memorable night out of it."

I summoned the waiter for our bill, then I paid and we skedaddled. The sultry night beckoned to us, and there were so many joints to choose from, each having live music, dancing, and drinks. The plethora of entertainment spots was just another reason why I was so in love with New Orleans. We walked, hand-in-hand, enjoying the atmosphere. On Frenchman Street, we heard a brass band playing funk, and I pulled Dolores inside the club where the music was coming from. The joint was packed, but not uncomfortably so. We jostled with others, and I led us to an empty space close to the bandstand.

We were both already feeling pretty mellow from the earlier drinks, and I quickly ordered a couple more from a passing waitress. We sipped our drinks, grinning at each other, the underlying heat between us coloring our thoughts. The beat of the drums and the low thrum of the bass hypnotized our bodies into unconsciously swaying and moving. By the second drink, Dolores and I were in our own little bubble. Dancing together, our bodies rubbing against each other, with sweat beginning to form on our grinding bodies. Our dancing became an imitation of the world's oldest dance, our midsections grinding rhythmically together. Looking into her eyes, I did what comes naturally in such a situation; I kissed her.

Her soft lips parted, welcoming my tongue into her mouth. Our tongues looped and whirled, our lips voraciously attacking each other, with our bodies as close together as they could be, separated only by our clothes. I needed to feel her nakedness against me, my need for her suddenly overwhelming. I sucked on her earlobe, then whispered to her, "Let's go."

She nodded, moaning into my neck. I grabbed her hand, dropped a couple of bills for the waitress, then we fled out of the club. We hailed a passing cab and jumped in. I quickly gave my address to the cab driver. Our cars could be retrieved later, because we were finally having our moment.

We kissed all during the taxi ride to my house and upon exiting we didn't even make it through the front door. Once the cab pulled away, we attacked each other, lips, mouths, hands, groping, and pulling. I opened her low cut blouse and freed the breasts which had been teasing me all evening. I put her left breast in my mouth and pulled her onto the porch swing where I had first seen her. Dolores unbuckled my pants and begin stroking my hardened length. I eased her skirt up, pulling her panties down. I pulled her onto my lap and entered her wetness. The porch swing aided our movements, and I smiled to myself as I pumped upwards into her volcanic womanhood. I enjoyed both of my graduation gifts at the same time.

# 23

# 11:59:40

I'm reflecting on my life while recounting my story. I'm realizing the points in my life where I should have gone left instead of right. I know hindsight is twenty-twenty, but I wish I'd have done some things a lot differently. Especially when it came to matters of the heart. I never got it right.

After a night of intense, yet tender, lovemaking, Dolores left in the morning after giving me a hug. I waved as her cab pulled away, wondering where our relationship would go from there. We had talked of our financial stuff, but even after making love three or four times, I still didn't have a clue as to what was next. I didn't get a chance to find out because Bobby took the decision out of my hands.

He called me not too long after Dolores had left. His tone was quite brisk, and I did my best to understand what he was telling me.

"Jackson, I need you to pack a suitcase, maybe even two," he said. "There's a business situation I need you to handle."

"Where am I going?" I asked. "And what do you want me to do, exactly?"

"You're going up north. You'll handle everything and the logistics will be given to you when necessary. It's a big deal, and consider it a test of your skills. Be at the airfield tomorrow morning at seven, and take a coat. I won't be there to look over your shoulder, so it's all on you. Pack for two weeks."

Then he hung up, and I sat there looking at the phone receiver in my hand. He was being coy, and I felt as if I were being dropped into a situation without having the ammo or necessary information to be successful. It was on purpose, I realized, and I put the receiver back in place, and started packing for a two-week business trip.

When I finished packing I sent Dolores a text explaining I'd be away for a little while. I figured I'd only be gone for a few days at most, so she and I could discuss whatever we needed to when I got back. Whatever we needed to discuss would keep and if not I would only be a phone call or text away. She didn't respond.

When a person has a flight booked on a private jet, the process is much different than when one is flying commercial. Personal cars will be parked a couple of hundred feet away from the landing strip, and then it's simple to just walk to the plane. It's one of those things in life I could definitely get used to. I knew it must be important if I were flying on a private plane, because it meant I wouldn't be alone on the flight.

Sure enough, when I parked my Cadillac I saw people scurrying to board the company jet. Bobby was standing on the tarmac, obviously waiting for me. I locked my car and walked to meet him. He extended his hand to me, then he started talking fast.

"Okay, we're going to acquire a global logistics company, and I need you to handle the numbers part of the deal," he said.

A pilot took my suitcase and loaded it under the plane. Bobby handed me a leather briefcase and walked to the stairs with me. I waited for him to climb the stairs, but he turned to look at me, a smile on his face, and a devilish look in the eyes which looked so much like mine.

"I'm not going with you because I have another project I'm working on," Bobby said. "The team I've assembled for this are all out of the Jackson office. Let them do their jobs, and you use your skill to find any holes, any leverage, and you make it happen. I'll talk to you daily, and we'll get this deal done."

"Where am I going?" I asked. I paused walking up the stairs, looking back at him.

"St. Louis. All of the info is in the briefcase, and you have a company laptop in there as well. Familiarize yourself with all of the details and nuances, then figure out how we're going to proceed. Have a good trip."

He patted me on the shoulder, then turned and started walking towards the parked cars. If it was such a big deal, why wasn't he going? What big project was he working on which could trump this mission I was being sent on? I needed information, but there was no one to ask. I had yet to form any close-knit business relationships with anyone at the company. I shrugged, because sometimes there are things one cannot control or predict.

Once I entered the plane the door was shut behind me, and the lone flight attendant showed me to my seat. I looked around at the five other passengers, who either nodded at me or ignored me. They all seemed to be busy reading paperwork, so I figured I needed to get caught up myself.

I read through the financials of Golden Logistics. It seemed to be financially sound, with many assets. The company had started off as a regional trucking company twenty years before, but they'd expanded into global shipping and air freight. Their headquarters was in St. Louis, but they had satellite offices in Mexico, California, and China. It seemed the current board of directors was ready to cash in and move on. I'd make it happen because I felt as if I were being tested, and it would be a lucrative deal which would pay dividends for decades. Freight is a necessary thing for every household or business, and Golden Logistics would hatch golden eggs, as far as I could tell.

I read everything there was in the briefcase, which included their assets, their financials, and their asking price. I'd crunch the numbers some more when I got to the hotel, and by the time we'd start our meeting with them the next day, I'd know how we needed to proceed.

I looked around at my fellow passengers, realizing I'd have to talk to them at some point. I'd have to find out what each of their specialties were in order to delegate when the negotiations started. I removed my seat belt and stood up.

"I need your attention for a couple of minutes," I said. My five fellow passengers stopped their activities and looked at me quizzically. "I should have introduced myself when we boarded the plane, but I needed to learn more about the purpose of this trip. I'm Rob Jackson, the CFO of Fitzgerald Industries. Maybe you've seen my name on an e-mail, and now you can match the name to a face."

I studied each person's face for a moment. I was looking for sneers or a surprised look, but their expressions did not change. Everyone seemed more interested in my words than the color of my skin. I felt myself relaxing because they would not pre-judge me.

When we get to our hotel, I want to see everyone in the hotel bar twenty minutes after check-in," I continued. "We'll become better acquainted, and we'll discuss the strategy for this acquisition. Thanks in advance."

I sat back down, and watched as they shared furtive looks with each other. Only one pair of eyes remained on me, those belonging to a pretty woman of about my age. As I returned her stare, she blushed and looked away. Curious behavior on her part, but maybe she found me attractive. Well, I wasn't a monk, but the feeling was mutual. I would wait and see.

We deplaned and a limousine was waiting to take us to

the hotel in the downtown area, not too far from the Gateway Arch. I introduced myself with a handshake to my compatriots, three men and two women. The men had generic names like James, John, and Bill. I figured I'd sort them out as we became better acquainted. The two women were Elaine, an older woman, and Susie, the blonde woman who'd been staring at me. Susie was about my age, but I noticed the wedding band on her finger. Pity, because Susie was a very attractive blonde with grayish-green eyes, and a nice figure. I looked at her body for a few extra seconds when we exited the limo. Susie was blessed with a curvaceous figure, and I envied her husband for a couple of seconds, and hoped the bastard knew how lucky he was to be able to enjoy her lushness. I thought of Dolores then, and wondered if we kept seeing each other in an intimate relationship, would matrimony be in our future? It was something to think about.

After checking in I deposited my suitcase in my room, and washed my face. I was still recovering from the night before with Dolores. Before leaving to join my colleagues, I sent Dolores a text message explaining more about my current situation. I assured her we would talk upon my return, because there were some personal things we needed to discuss, as well as business items. I also messaged her to keep an eye on Golden Logistics, just in case there was more information to be found. Satisfied, I put away the phone, and headed downstairs.

The group was waiting for me in the hotel bar. They were sitting at a back table, which was really two tables pushed together. They'd all brought their briefcases, as if this was going to be a quiz. I already knew what I needed to know about Golden, but I needed to know what the team thought in order to delegate responsibilities. Chess.

"We know what Golden wants, as far as cash, but we aren't going to pay their price, we're going to pay our price," I said. "Before this night is over, we'll know how to use their weaknesses against them. Let's get to work. Oh, and the drinks are on me to midnight."

My last sentence seemed to relax them, putting them at ease. They each ordered drinks, and I opened up a tab. Somehow, sweet-smelling Susie sat next to me. It was hard to concentrate with her alluring scent messing up my concentration, but I managed. It wasn't easy.

By midnight our strategy was in place. James would make our initial offer, John would ask for more time, and Susie would hit them with the numbers which would make them pause to consider our offer. Meanwhile, Bill and Elaine would make visits and contact twenty of Golden's biggest customers whose contracts were expiring. Their job was to convince those customers to let the contracts lapse, with an agreement from us to resign for lower rates after the acquisition went through. I would silently quarterback the whole operation.

I had cut off everyone's drinks at 11:45, and at 11:59, I settled up the tab. I bade everyone good night, and told them to be sharp for the next day's events. I checked my phone for a message from Dolores, but there was nothing. I sent Bobby a message telling him I had it under control and if he had any questions, to call me. Bobby sent a text back immediately, saying he would.

I walked towards the bank of elevators and Susie was there, chattering vehemently on her cell phone. As I stepped closer, she slammed it closed with a vengeance.

"Fucker," she said. Then she saw me standing there. "Oh, sorry about you witnessing my ranting, but my ex-husband has to be the dumbest sack of shit ever born."

"You don't look old enough to be married, let alone divorced," I said. I wanted to find out more about her, but I didn't want to appear too nosy.

"It only lasted a year, because he was an idiot. I only married him because my father sort of pushed us together," Susie said. "But I'm going to keep wearing my ring, because it keeps deadbeats away."

I nodded my head at the wisdom of her statement, because her ring had given me pause as well. I definitely would not mind helping her get over her divorce in the only way I knew how, but business came first. Pity.

"We're going to be in St. Louis for a couple of weeks at least," I said. "The deal won't be done overnight, so we may as well enjoy ourselves. Tomorrow night, after our evening group chat, why don't you go out for drinks with me?"

Susie smiled at me, blushing a little bit. "I'd love to. I've never been in St. Louis before, and I'd love to explore it while I'm here."

"Neither have I," I said. "I look forward to discovering it together. I'll see you in the morning."

Suddenly, I wasn't in any hurry to get back to New Orleans and Dolores. St. Louis might turn out to be fun after all.

# 24

# 11:59:41

The prettiest sweater in the world becomes worthless when it begins to unravel. A dangling thread always begs for us to pull it, just to see what will happen. Then in the blink of an eye our sweater, or life as it may be, loses all value. Our beautiful, perfect lives are held together by only so many dangling threads. Snip, snip, snip, game over.

The acquisition meeting went pretty much how I thought it would. We thrust, and they parried, but in the end they agreed to meet with us three days later. I kept Bobby abreast of the situation, and my troops sallied forth in the directions I'd pointed them in. I was determined to get this deal done. I wanted to make my mark at Fitzgerald Industries because I wanted to be the CEO someday.

Meanwhile, sweet-smelling Susie was on my mind. I didn't know what the situation with Dolores would be when I returned home, because her few texts to me had consisted of one-word responses, such as "Yes" or "Okay." When I called her she didn't answer the phone. I didn't know whether or not she regretted sleeping with me, but life is too short to wait for someone else to make up their minds.

I had convinced Susie to go out for drinks with me, away from the hotel and the rest of the team. I had never dated or slept with anyone I'd worked with before, so I was making sure there was no harassment involved. The Dolores situation occurred after we'd mutually agreed she no longer worked for me. Workplace romances can turn into tornadoes of shit if not handled correctly. I prided myself on being a great chess player, so I needed to be cautious with Susie.

We went to a bar and grill in the downtown area, within walking distance of the hotel. Susie told me about herself as we walked. She was from Mississippi, but had split her childhood between her divorced parents. She was a numbers whiz, and she'd gotten her accounting degree from Ol' Miss. She'd married soon after, relocating to Jackson to work for Fitzgerald Industries. Her husband's family had been friends of her father's, so it had been mostly an arranged marriage. It had fizzled quickly as she concentrated more on her career. The divorce had only been finalized recently, but she said she was looking forward to an unencumbered life.

I let her information settle itself into my mind, and I knew Susie might be ripe for the same desires as me. No relationship, just fun. I think her words led me to my decision as to what I should do about Dolores. Dolores and I could do business together, maybe even be casual lovers, but I wanted to be rich and in charge. A wife and kids weren't on my agenda. Not then. Why not enjoy sweet smelling Susie and her delicious body?

We started off with tequila shots, chased with beer. I sensed Susie really hadn't been out for a while, so I was determined to make sure she had a good time, whether we ended up in bed or not. I told jokes, and we sang along to the music blaring from the jukebox. We even danced a couple of times, but I maintained a safe distance. I didn't want to scare her away with the weight of my amorous intentions pressing against her body. I wanted her to make the first move, then I would take over from there.

Around midnight, we started walking back towards the hotel. On a whim we detoured and headed toward the river, hand in hand. It was a peaceful night, and the only other people we saw were couples walking together, as we were. The full moon was perfectly reflected on the black water of the Mississippi, and I felt so peaceful then. Slightly tipsy, and holding the hand of a sexy woman. Our eyes locked, and Susie tilted her head and kissed me full on the mouth. I kissed her back just as sweetly and softly, but the softness didn't last. Her kisses became more violent, more inviting, turning me on to the point where I ignored place and time. Against the wall of one of the buildings along the river, we manhandled each other, caught up in the moment. I pushed her business skirt up, and my fingers began to play inside of her panties, stroking her womanhood. Wetness oozed over my fingers, and I freed myself from my pants. I lifted her up against the wall and I plunged the length of me inside of her. Moaning, panting, kissing, sucking, nibbling, thrusting, a whirlwind of sex between two passionate people lost in each other. Susie experienced multiple orgasms, and with each spasm, she dug her nails deeper into my back. With a furious bellow, I emptied myself into her, and we rested there, against the wall, until we were able to move again.

Straightening out our clothes we kissed gently, before walking back to the hotel. Before entering the lobby, we discussed the business plans for tomorrow. Her job was to do research, while other members attended to their designated jobs. I'd crunch some more numbers, readying our offer for the next meeting.

"Okay, so I know what I have to do tomorrow," she said. "I can sleep in, and work from my hotel room. Want to join me for a nightcap?"

Her lips were parted in anticipation, and my body said "yes" to those lips. We caught separate elevators to her floor and I spent the night in her room discovering all I could about the sweet-smelling and sexual dynamo, Susie. I explored her nakedness from behind, from above, and enjoyed every second of it. I left not an inch of her undiscovered.

I left her room around five in the morning, smiling at the image of her sleeping, naked body. For the next two weeks I made love to Susie every day, while still maintaining a business-only façade to the rest of the world. We treated each other with indifference around the team, and we made sure not to give anything away. We were enthralled with each other, and the sex was mind-blowing.

The moves I'd orchestrated with the team had Golden Logistics capitulating to our offer. They knew it was in their best interest to acquiesce to our offer, and they agreed to our terms. Their entire board signed the paper-work we'd presented to them, and the only thing left to do was to arrange the wire transfers. I'd achieved what I'd set out to do, adding more luster to the reputation I was building at Fitzgerald Industries.

I called Bobby and told him the good news. The ball was in his court then, because I'd done my job and then some. The acquisition took place for sixty million dollars less than Golden's original request. Bobby told me the entire team would receive bonuses based on the money we'd saved. He didn't ask any other questions, only telling me he'd arranged for me to fly back on a commercial airline because the company jet was in New York. It wouldn't be a problem, I assured him. I was just ready to be home in New Orleans.

I made furious love to Susie, or what I thought of as goodbye sex. Lying in bed with her, spent from our marathon, we discussed the possibilities and repercuss-sions, because we knew we'd probably run into each other at some point working for the same company. There were no percentages in promises, nor did we need to try and have a relationship, we both agreed. Either way, we'd enjoyed each other's company and each other's bodies.

There was nothing for us to regret. We hugged before I left her room, thankful we'd had the experience we'd shared.

Upon my return to New Orleans I called Dolores, trying to get in contact with her, but to no avail. I couldn't figure out how to fix the problem if I didn't know there was one. She didn't return my texts either, and when I went to the office space we'd shared, the sign on the door said "For Rent." Stunned, I did the only thing I could think of; I called Ms. Lenora.

Ms. Lenora greeted me warmly, then she gave me information which floored me.

"My baby fell in love with you a long time ago, Jackson. She knows you better than anyone. Dolores knows you're not in love with her, so she's running away from you," Ms. Lenora said. "She'll be in touch with you, when she lands, I guess. Hopefully she'll be in contact soon, but she's mailed all paperwork to you, and deposited whatever monies due to you. Keep focusing on where you're trying to go, and it'll all work out for you."

I thanked Ms. Lenora, offering my apologies. She assured me it wasn't my fault, because we can't control who falls in love with us. She hung up, assuring me Dolores would be in touch when she was ready.

I sat on my porch swing, rocking and thinking. I hadn't recognized Dolores was in love with me, because I didn't know what love was supposed to look like. My relationship with Octavia had been more friendship based, as opposed to being in love. Would I have done anything differently if I'd known? I'd be haunted by that question for the rest of my life. I should have been able to recognize what being in love looked like, but how could I when I'd never seen love on display? I'd missed out on an opportunity to be normal, or in love with an amazing woman I could have built a future with. It hadn't been meant to be. Love, the greatest mystery in life, didn't seem to want to be a friend to me.

## 25

## 11:59:44

The first nine holes of golf aren't the most important. Holes ten through eighteen are where legends are made, where greatness is personified, and where the game is won or lost. So far, I've told the tale of my first nine holes, a couple of bogies, a few birdies, and a couple of pars. The back nine is where I tended to bogey a lot.

The next four or five months were a blur of business trips, meetings, and sleepless nights. Dolores had sent me all the paperwork regarding all of our business, and she'd deposited profits into my account. Ms. Lenora would only say, "She's fine," when I called. I had to settle for what I could. The partnership and the relationship were over. Life happens.

Bobby sent me an email requesting my presence at a board meeting, where he'd announce his retirement, his replacement, and other monumental changes taking place at Fitzgerald Industries. I was surprised he was going to retire, but I was excited I would finally be getting my chance. I was the next in line, as far as I knew, and I'd been great in my position since I'd gotten it. The investment portfolio was growing, new business was pouring in, and I was responsible for a lot of it. I would finally get my chance to shine. The only issue I had was the location of the meeting, which was in Jackson, Mississippi.

I hadn't been in the state of Mississippi since I'd left on the train going north to Boniface many years before. Now I was being summoned back, and I should have felt exhilaration instead of trepidation. I packed a suitcase, a cooler for my soft drinks, my briefcase, and my laptop, into the Cadillac. It's only a three-and-a-half-hour drive from New Orleans to Jackson, so I figured I might as well put my car on the highway. I didn't know how long I'd be required to stay, but I'd like to have my car close by, in case I needed it for a quick escape.

*Welcome to Mississippi*, the sign read as I crossed the border on I-55 North. I stopped once for a sandwich at a gas station, and I felt as if all eyes were on me. I looked the picture of the well-to-do young urban professional, but I was in enemy territory. Old men driving rusted pick-up trucks with Confederate flag license plates eyed me suspiciously, making me feel as if I were guilty of shoplifting or something. No, my only crime was the duskiness of my skin. I hurried back to the security of my car, and I got back on the highway.

An hour later, I pulled into the parking lot of the Fitzgerald Industries complex. In the years I'd been working for Fitzgerald, I'd managed to avoid coming to this place, partly because Bobby knew how much I hated Mississippi. Yet I'd been forced back here. I cheered myself by thinking how I'd switch the headquarters to New Orleans as soon as they made me the CEO. I had a fleeting thought of Susie, and I wondered how she was. Maybe I'd look her up while I was here. It couldn't hurt.

I was met in the lobby by a suited young man who seemed to have been waiting specifically for me. He escorted me to the second floor conference room, where the Board of Directors was waiting. My seat was toward the head of the table, befitting my position. The chair at the head of the table was empty, waiting for Bobby to sit in it. There were two other empty chairs, one next to the head, and the other one to my left. The murmuring was low and continuous, hushing only when Bobby appeared in the room. The table stood up and applauded his appearance, quieting down only when he bade them to. He remained standing, while gesturing for everyone else to sit down. I gave him a nod of recognition when his eyes locked on mine. He gave an almost imperceptible nod, before looking away.

"Thanks for the applause, you make me feel pretty good about myself," Bobby said. "I've been the CEO of Fitzgerald Industries for almost thirty years, and it's time for me to step aside and let the future begin. Before I name my replacement, I want to announce another promotion. I've chosen a new Chief Operating Officer, and it'll make history. She'll be the first woman with that kind of clout at this company. Let me reiterate something—nobody ever gave her anything since she's been here. Let me introduce your new COO, Susanna Whitman."

Susie walked into the room, or rather waddled into the room. She was hugely pregnant, which made my mind start counting backwards to St. Louis. How many months pregnant was she? Susie made her way around the table, shaking some hands, hugging other men. When she got to the chair next to me, I pulled it out for her. She hugged me, then whispered in my ear, "We'll talk later, I promise."

I smiled, pleased at the thought of having a conversation with Susie, yet I also had a quivering in my stomach thinking about me possibly being the father of Susie's impending miracle. Fatherhood was an abstract thought, something I'd never seriously considered. How good of a father could I be? Especially as I'd never had a father to emulate. I looked at my father standing at the head of the table, smiling at the applause. *He was such a shining example of fatherhood*, I thought sarcastically.

Once Susie was seated, Bobby began to talk again.

"She's come a long way since she used to run around my office in pigtails, right?" Bobby said, beaming at her, his grayish-green eyes meeting her grayish-green eyes. My sandwich tried to erupt out of my stomach, but somehow, maybe through sheer will, I didn't vomit.

Susie was Bobby's daughter, which made her my

sister by blood. I sincerely hoped her baby wasn't mine.

# 26

# 11:59:45

When a shit storm starts swirling, it's almost impossible to stop it. All a person can do is hope the avalanche of shit does not bury them and disable them from being able to dig their way out. Our actions don't necessarily dictate the onset of a shit storm, but I swear they aren't brought on by karma. Take me, for instance. I prided myself on being nice and respectful to everyone, yet look at how well it worked out for me. Shit storms were not new to me.

I sat there in the boardroom, frozen. Susie's scent, which had turned me on so much in St. Louis, was now making me nauseous in Mississippi. Bobby was still standing up, waiting for the cacophony to subside. Once the room quieted down, Bobby Fitzgerald Jr. began to talk again.

"For the last few years, I've been quietly grooming my replacement," he said. "I've taught him everything I know, and he's taught me some things I didn't know." His eyes moved slowly around the table, before settling on mine. This was my moment. This would be the culmination of all I'd ever dreamt of, my reward for the years of suffering at Boniface, the loneliness I'd endured since the death of my mother. My father was going to pass the torch to me, his son. His eyes looked away from me.

"Your new CEO will be my son," he said. "Robert Fitzgerald III."

The room erupted as the young demigod walked in, tan, fit, blond, and white. He shook hands with everyone, smiling and patting people on the shoulder. He hugged his sister, then he shook my hand, smiling as he looked into my eyes, which were identical to his own. Robert went to the head of the table, where he bear hugged his father before sitting in the chair at the head of the table. *Long live the king*, I thought bitterly.

"Jackson will continue on as CFO, and the three of them will guide our company to new heights," Bobby said. "I'll continue on as a Board member, but effective immediately, I am done. Meeting adjourned."

I remained seated as did Robert and Susie. The rest of the Board members shook Robert's hand, and I half expected them to kiss his ring. While others were saying their goodbyes, I quietly turned to Susie and I asked her.

"Is it mine, Susie?" I asked. She nodded in affirmation, and before she could begin to explain, I put my finger to her lips. "I'm sorry, Susie. I'll do whatever you need me to do, but I won't be allowed to be a daddy to your child," I said. At the quizzical look on her face, I shook my head negatively. "I'll only tell the story once."

After the last Board member left, I walked to the door and closed it, locking it because I didn't want any disturbances. Rage was pulsing through me, causing my hands to shake. I willed myself to keep my emotions under control—no easy task considering the circumstances.

Bobby Jr. was standing at the head of the table, smiling, as if he had the world on a string, which I guess he thought he did.

"Robert," I said to my brother, causing him to direct his attention to me. "Congratulations. I'm sure you feel as if you earned it, but I beg to differ. I am the one who garnered the Golden Logistics acquisition. I am the one who's boosted the profits since I've been here. And now, you'll reap the benefits and the credit, but it's always been like that. Right, Bobby? Or should I say Dad or Father? What does a person call their biological father who never showed them any kind of love?"

Susie gasped as understanding dawned on her face, causing her to slump down in her chair. Robert looked puzzled, and Bobby Jr. had turned pale, looking as if he were ready to puke.

"Robert, don't do this," Bobby Jr. said. His son Robert looked completely confused by this exchange, not knowing who his father, yes, his father, was referring to.

"I don't answer to Robert. I never have and never will. I hate it and I refuse to let anyone call me by your name," I said calmly. "Funny, three Roberts in one room, all named after the same person. Call me Jackson, or call me nothing at all, but today is my last day here at Fitzgerald Industries. All I have ever been to you is a new kind of nigger. Not in the kitchen or in the fields, but in boardrooms and banks, keeping everything clean and tidy for Massa's family. Well, that shit is over, as far as I'm concerned. Tomorrow morning, I'll need ten million dollars wired into my account. Otherwise, the nation's newspapers will have a field day with our family story."

Bobby was apoplectic, his face turning red. "No one will care! Sure, people may point fingers, but our situation is not too different from other people's stories," he said.

"Well, I hate to be the bearer of bad news, but your two oldest children are about to be parents," I said. I began laughing at the stupid look on Bobby Jr.'s face. "Parents of the same child, Bobby. It'll look as if you're breeding your children like the Pharaohs of Egypt. It won't go over so well in the American South, Bob."

I didn't look at Susie, because I didn't want to feel compassion or pity for anyone right then. I pulled a pen out and wrote down my account number which I'd memorized years before. I handed the piece of paper to Robert, who looked as if he'd rather be anyplace else in the world.

"Call it a bonus or a buyout, Robert, it doesn't matter to me," I said. I gathered my things in preparation to leave the room. "Susie, I swear I didn't know. I will contact you so I can set up a financial arrangement. Bobby, we're finally done."

Tears were rolling down Susie's face, but I hadn't intended to cause them. The blame could honestly be lain at the feet of her father, but he was too busy scheming and planning to realize he'd not protected his kingdom as much as he should have.

I unlocked the door, then I looked fully into the face of the man whose blood flowed through my veins. He was ashen, with disbelief written across his pitiful face.

"Checkmate," I said.

Then I left the building and jumped into my car, ready to get the fuck out of Mississippi.

# 27

# 11:59:46

Leaving burned bridges behind means a person can only go forward. Sometimes we have to destroy the things that keep us tethered to the past. Otherwise, we'd be stuck, dooming ourselves to never achieving all that we could. Burn them down, and then focus on the road ahead.

Since I'd first realized I had a head for business, I'd had a secret dream of being completely in charge of Fitzgerald Enterprises. That was it. I hadn't thought about anything else, as far as a path to the destination of my choosing. I'd worked my ass off to get the top spot, but it wasn't meant to be. Now I had to create a new plan, to find something I was not only good at, but something I'd enjoy. I had money in the bank, and shit, if I wanted to, I could have gone to Jackson Square daily and played chess for money. It was too easy to do that, and I'd never taken or been given an easy path to anything. I'd find something to invest in, or maybe I'd venture into something new. I wasn't an artist, painter, or writer, so being a creative was out. Maybe I would look around at restaurants or bars. There was no real hurry or pressure from anyone other than myself. I wasn't used to not having a goal in mind before I embarked on a personal quest. I would figure something out, something which would inflame my passions. I would see.

Ten million dollars was wired into my account the next day. So, at least one of my dreams had come true. I was officially rich, but now what? Everything I'd been doing since I'd arrived at Boniface had led me to this point. My only real skill was making money, and I wanted to take a break from the world of finance for awhile.

I thought of traveling, but I really didn't want to go alone. I had no one again, and I began feeling sorry for myself. I attempted one vacation, a week in San Francisco. I considered calling Melanie, but she was located in Los Angeles, which is pretty far from San Francisco. I drank the whole week I was there. I drank at Fisherman's Wharf, feeling apathetic about my life going forward. On the ferry to Alcatraz, I found myself vomiting into the choppy water of the San Francisco Bay. By the time the ferry docked on the island, I was empty, both physically and mentally. I toured the prison, saddened by the size of the cells. Men had spent their whole adult lives in those tiny cubicles, caged like animals. I couldn't imagine it, knowing my love of freedom. I'd rather die than spend my life caged up.

The Napa Valley tour gave me an appreciation for wine which I hadn't had before. I'd drank wine on my European vacation, but I'd been so young I could have been drinking flavored gasoline and I wouldn't have cared. After sampling so many wines in the Napa Valley, I decided on the spot to have a wine cellar built in my Garden District house. At least I'd have something to focus on while I figured out my next move.

Upon returning to New Orleans, I applied for a library card. I was still the consummate student, and I taught myself how to build a wine rack in my house. Since I didn't have a basement or a cellar, I turned an unused pantry into a pretty spiffy wine room. Reading and drinking wine became my drugs for the next eight months. And I reignited my passion for chess.

I'd wake up in the morning, eat a small breakfast and read till around noon. I'd get my chess bag, consisting of a board and the pieces, then I'd make my way to a local park where people met to play chess. There'd be gambling on the games, sometimes as much as fifty dollars. I'd win a lot, losing rarely. The money I'd win was used to buy groceries, beer, supplies, and whiskey. I drank about a fifth a week, but I never got drunk. Just melancholy. Interestingly enough, I had more money in the bank than I'd ever dreamt of, but it didn't bring me any happiness, as I'd often thought it would. I needed to figure out what I needed to do to bring happiness and balance to my life. One day, I made a phone call. Susie answered on the third ring.

"Susie, there are things we need to discuss," I said. "First, let me apologize for a couple of things. I'm normally not the sort of person to indulge in one-night stands, nor am I careless. I was careless in our encounters, and I'm extremely sorry. The second thing is I want to be involved in my child's life, not just a DNA contributor. I grew up without a father, and I don't want to make the same mistakes our father did. Is that something you'll be all right with?"

"For the record, you weren't the only careless one," she said. "It takes two, and we both played a part in it. It would be easy to blame tequila, or you, or even our father for not telling us about each other. It feels weird to say 'our father.' Jackson, we can't push the rewind button on anything that's happened, but we can make the future as bright as possible for our child. Yes, I want you in his life, and to some extent in mine, as well. We can move forward from this because we are both to be blamed, yet we are blameless, if that makes any sense. We didn't know. Now we do. I'd like to get to know you, because we'll be in each other's lives from now on."

I told her my entire life story, going back to my childhood. When I described my mother's death, I could hear Susie crying on the other end. I detailed my Boniface experience, my relationship with Octavia, and the role Bobby Jr. played in everything. Our conversation lasted two hours as we talked of our different upbringings, and the things we wanted for our child. By the time Susie and I ended our conversation, I could see that our child would be all right with us as co-parents.

Liam Jackson Fitzgerald was born healthy. The dusky hue of his skin proclaimed his racial mix. Susie called me right after he'd been born, and a week later his first pictures were hanging on my refrigerator. The time of his birth was a heavy drinking period for me, as I toasted his birth and lamented it at the same time. Poor baby. Idly I wondered what Bobby Jr. was feeling about his new grandson. If he wasn't happy about it, he had no one to blame but himself.

A month or so later, there was a knock upon the front entrance. I was puzzled because the only time someone knocked at my address was if I'd ordered a pizza or if it was a salesman. Skeptically, I walked toward the door, looking through the panes to see who it was. I didn't see anyone, so maybe they'd left. I opened the doors and stepped out, looking up the driveway to see if someone was walking back toward the street.

"Hey, Jackson," a familiar voice said.

Sitting in my porch swing, where I'd first met her, was Dolores. She wasn't alone, though. She was holding a wiggling baby, who was seemingly not impressed with the swaying of the swing. I was speechless at the sight of her, wanting to hug her, but I restrained myself.

"Hey Dolores, come on in," I said. I held the door open for her and the baby. "What's the baby's name?" I asked.

"His name is Jasper Robert Jackson," she said.

My mouth was agape, stunned by her statement. We'd only slept together one night, leaving me somewhat skeptical about me being the baby's father. Trust was something I did not possess in abundance. I led them to the kitchen, not even thinking of why I led them there. I made sure she was comfortable, then I waited for her explanation.

"The night we made love was one of the best nights of my life," she said. "I'd finally made love with the man I was in love with, and I floated on cloud nine for a while. Then you left for St. Louis, and I realized it wasn't reciprocal. You loved me, but not in the way I wanted you to. In my fear of being hurt, I abandoned ship."

"Where'd you go?" I asked. "Your mother wouldn't tell me your whereabouts."

"I packed all of my stuff and had it shipped to my mother's house in Arizona. I then liquidated all of our accounts, giving you your share," she said. "I followed my stuff a week or so later to my mother's house, and I cried in her arms upon arrival."

I sat there, feeling like shit. Everything Dolores said was true, and I felt horrible. It was too late to mend the fence between us. I looked at her baby, Jasper.

"When did you find out you were pregnant?" I asked.

"A month after I arrived at my mother's. My father wanted you to be informed, but my mother said the time wasn't right," Dolores said. "I'd quietly started rebuilding my life, leasing office space, and garnering the appropriate licenses and such. My parents said I could stay with them, and when Jasper came, my mother fell in love with him. Would you like to hold him?"

It dawned on me then I'd never held a baby before. I was almost thirty years old and this simple thing had never been part of my life. I reached for him, while

Dolores gave me instructions on how to support his head. I looked into his funny-colored eyes, and I knew. Jasper Robert Jackson was my son, just as Liam was. Ironic how a fatherless boy now had two boys of his own.

"Why the name Jasper?" I asked, thinking of the old man who had taken me to two funerals and watched my life from afar.

"Because Jasper always looked out for you, according to my mother," she replied. "He was a very nice man, and he loved you and your mother. It felt right."

"Grab the picture off of the refrigerator," I said. "I have a story of my own to tell."

Dolores pulled Liam's picture from beneath the refrigerator magnet and looked at me, astonished.

"Yes, he's my son, Liam," I said. I then told her the entire sordid story of the sexual escapades of my sister Susie and me, minus the explicit details. I detailed Bobby Jr.'s final betrayal, and my rebuttal. I found myself telling Dolores of how useless I felt, and how I'd run out of ideas.

She looked at me, watching me rock my son. Then she started smiling.

"Well, you'd better come up with something, because you have two sons to look after," she said.

Dolores was right. Whether I had wanted my sons in this world or not, they were here through no fault of their own. I had to give this fatherhood thing my best effort. Unlike the two men who'd been my fathers in name and in blood, my sons would know they were loved and cherished by their father.

Dolores and I sat up talking until late in the night. I'd

even sent Susie a message telling her about Jasper. I told Susie she could bring Liam to New Orleans once a month, so he could get to know his father. I informed Susie and Dolores no matter what else happened in the world, I wanted my sons to know they were brothers, and I asked them both to allow them the comfort of each other. With tears dripping from her eyes, Dolores agreed. Susie messaged me saying she'd make sure Liam and Jasper spent time together. For the first time in my life, I felt as if my cup was running over with blessings. I felt the darkness leaving my soul, replaced by the unfamiliar light of hope.

Dolores and Jasper spent the night in a guestroom, but I couldn't sleep. I was thinking of train sets, fishing expeditions, teaching my sons how to ride bikes, and play catch. Dolores, my graduation gift, had brought me two more gifts with her. My son Jasper, and my mojo. I had gotten it back.

# 28

## 11:59:49

The pause button doesn't seem to be working for me right now, and the force of inevitability marches closer. The road less travelled turned out to be just as fucked up as the easy path. What defines easy, though? The easy way must be to just stand still, scared to move forward with this whole life thing. I'll admit, fear of the unknown which awaits me, has me quaking in my bones.

With changed focus, I re-entered life after the boys were born. I was reinvigorated by the fact of my children's existence, which led me to upgrade all of the at-home technology I owned. I had the knowledge and skill required to do well at day trading, which would allow me to work from home. I didn't need the money, but I needed ways to occupy my time. I set a schedule for myself, which I adhered to strictly. I'd get up in the morning, shower and get dressed as if I were going to a regular job. To be successful in any endeavor, one has to treat it as a profession. Whether it's as a writer, painter, chef, or a musician, a professional routine keeps a person focused, even if their profession is their passion. It's what separates greatness from mediocrity.

By 6:45 every morning I was sitting in front of my computer, waiting for the stock market to open. With a cup of coffee in my hand or in front of me, I'd review reports and trends from the day before, making sure my ducks were in a row before I started buying and selling. It was like a global chess game, planned positioning being very important in this field just as in chess.

I'd take a lunch break around noon, usually consisting of soup or a sandwich. I wasn't a culinary wizard by any means, but I could cook enough to get by. Usually around two o'clock I'd knock off for the day, unless something out of the ordinary was brewing, which meant I'd be frantically buying and selling until the bell rang, ending the business day. At six P.M every night, I would make my two phone calls religiously. On the weekends I might only call on Sunday mornings, but on the weekdays, without fail, I called Susie and Dolores.

Susie was doing well as the COO at Fitzgerald, but she was wearing the hat I had used to wear. She and Robert had agreed to eliminate the CFO position, splitting the duties between them. She'd offer some tips as to the directions they were going in as a company, but I never used any of the information to buy or sell stocks. I didn't need to or want to, disassociating myself from anything to do with Fitzgerald Industries. We'd talk about Liam or her unwillingness to date anyone, which was what I was experiencing myself. The mother of my child, my sister, had become a friend. So far Liam was a typical baby, showing no ill effects from his parents being so closely related. I would always keep my fingers crossed and my prayers sent that he would be normal for the rest of his life.

Dolores and I would follow mostly the same routine, discussing business and Jasper. The difference between the two daily conversations was I didn't want to know whether or not she was dating. I wished her every happiness, but I didn't care to witness whether or not she was in a happy, fulfilling relationship. It wasn't purely out of jealousy, but more out of regret. I don't know whether I could have ever loved her as she once had loved me, but I regretted not taking the chance before my life went in another direction. We were good at being friends, amazing as business partners, and our one night together had been unforgettable. I felt it was best to be co-parents, with no mention or hint about our lost possibilities.

My sons were three weeks apart in age, so their advances and progress were pretty much on the same level and at the same pace. They each got their first tooth and took their first steps at roughly the same time. Susie drove Liam to New Orleans once a month, and I'd visit with my son at my house, while she did whatever she felt like doing. I finally understood the sacrifices Flora Jean had made for me. She'd wanted me to grow up in a safe and stable environment, which explained everything. I wished she were present to see her grandsons, who she could have sung to and cuddled. She would have been a natural at being a grandmother.

They were amazing to behold. Jasper was a smiling, happy baby, whose grin could make me smile no matter what else was on my mind. Liam was a pistol, constantly running, curious about everything he could touch or see. I looked at them, thankful I had them, no matter how they had come to be. There's a saying, "God don't make no mistakes." I understood, because being able to hold and watch my two little boys in action was a true blessing, especially for someone like me, who'd missed out on the father-and-son relationship. I think my smile stayed on my face for a week after both of my boys uttered their first word. They both said, "Dada." My heart was theirs.

I journeyed to Arizona once a month to visit Jasper. The first time I visited, Ms. Lenora must've hugged me for about five minutes. I shook hands with her husband, Will, who probably nursed his own dark thoughts about me. Maybe time would soften his views of me. Dolores was breathtaking as usual, but I had no amorous intentions regarding us. We were co-parents, period. I'd root for her in all of her endeavors, as she would me.

Oh, and there's one more thing about the monthly trips to Arizona. I insisted on driving there. I still had the same Cadillac because cars didn't thrill me to the point where I needed to buy one, simply because I had the money. I'd rather use my money to add layers to the foundation of wealth I was building for my kids. It takes a day to drive across Texas, so if a person doesn't have to drive, then my advice would be to take a plane. I liked it because I didn't have to be bothered with trying to get flights, or dealing with the hustle and bustle of an international airport.

There's also a level of peace and contentment which comes with being on the highways across vast open spaces. The trip to Arizona averaged about a day and a half each way, and I wasn't one of those drivers who drives as if their hair were on fire. I took it nice and easy all the way. I'd have the air-conditioning on while music played, and the Cadillac ate up the miles. I always treated the monthly trips like a mini-vacation. I stopped at roadside diners for breakfast and lunch, and if I got sleepy I'd pull into a rest area or a truck stop for a short nap. I also did a lot of thinking and reflecting on those trips, and sometimes, I found myself with ideas which wouldn't go away.

My life was routine and normal, and I thought I was content. For a solid year and a half I traded stocks, watched my boys grow, and felt as if my life was pretty good. Then one day, on my return trip from Arizona, I got a bug up my ass about finding something new to do, something more exciting than trading stocks. I played with ideas, and as I passed a billboard advertising a chain pizza restaurant, an epiphany hit me. I thought of how great the pizza was in Chicago, and I thought a Chicago-style restaurant might do fine in a city where every restaurant seemed to serve Creole and Cajun food.

With my typical research and business acumen, I

found a location, not far from the French Market. It had been a restaurant at some point, and the space was good for what I envisioned. I bought the place, because to my thinking it's always better to own, not rent or lease. As I oversaw the renovations, my plan became more and more clear. It would not be a typical New Orleans restaurant, but a different kind of joint which sold authentic food from other parts of the country. It cost me a bit of money to open my joint up, but I felt the end result was worth every penny.

One thing I've found to be true about Chicago—it's impossible to duplicate their pizzas anywhere else. The recipes can't even be replicated because the pH levels of the water in Lake Michigan is different from anywhere else. So, I made a deal with four famous pizza joints there to ship me frozen pizza dough on a weekly basis. It was cheaper than having the water shipped in barrels, which allowed me to use my imagination to create a small, simple, and excellent menu.

My restaurant sold Chicago-style pizza, hot dogs, and Italian beef sandwiches, New England clam chowder, lobster rolls, and Texas-style chili. Those simple dishes comprised my entire menu, and I made a killing from the first day we opened the doors. Every restaurant in New Orleans seemed to sell the same types of food, and I created my own niche.

My restaurant, Lee Jasper's, featured a bar, an outdoor beer garden, and live music on Thursday nights and Sunday afternoons. I had fifteen employees working two shifts, but I was not content with only being the owner. I was hands-on with my restaurant most days, from the time we opened up at eleven in the morning, until we closed the place at midnight. I even started doing my day trading on my laptop, while drinking a beer in the outdoor beer garden once we opened. I was content in all the ways which counted, because life was finally giving me lemonade instead of lemons.

I'd get to Lee Jasper's about ten every morning, to make sure everything was set for the lunch crowd. On pretty days, I'd immediately go to the beer garden and set up my work station. I always sat at the same table, one which would let me keep an eye on everything happening at the restaurant, while allowing me to see the people walking by. I loved it, and my home office was for the weekends when I had father duty.

One week, I noticed a young woman of around my age set up her laptop and spend a couple of hours drinking beer, nibbling pizza, and utilizing the snazzy computer and her phone. She seemed to have the same type of lifestyle as me, which piqued my curiosity. She showed up every day, like clockwork, as if coming to Lee Jasper's was her job, like it was mine.

She was gorgeous in every way imaginable, and I could become hypnotized by looking at her. Her form-fitting sundresses and three-inch heels showcased the lushness of her body. Her round, heavy breasts sat up, with no hint of sag, accentuated by her slim waist. Her dresses hinted at perfect thighs, spotlighting her perfectly shaped calves, and a round, plump backside.

She was a light-skinned woman, about my complexion, which made me wonder about her racial make-up. Was she a mixture of two races? Or was she a masterpiece comprised of only one racial background? There was a fetching spray of freckles across her face which added to her allure, and to my eyes she was phenomenal in all the ways a woman could be.

I gave her a lot of visual attention, and to my delight she did not wear a wedding ring. She would sit down at her table, where she would arrange a laptop, setting her phone next to it. Her last move was the icing on an already impressive dessert; she'd open her purse, remove an eyeglass case, and put on a pair of reading glasses. I'd been out of the dating pool for a long time and I think it was the glasses which finally forced me out of my comfort zone. The glasses added to her sexiness, lending a nerdy quality to an already impressive package, similar to the vision of the world's sexiest librarian.

Finally, I couldn't take it anymore. She was sitting at her usual table, wearing a pair of linen shorts with a matching top, and a pair of high heels which strapped around her calves. I closed my laptop, and slowly approached her table. She shaded her eyes with her hand, while squinting up at me.

"Hey, how are you?" I asked." Do you mind if I keep you company for a while?"

She smiled at me, which I took as an affirmation or invitation, and I sat down facing her. I made it my business not to glance at her cleavage, because I didn't want to appear to be a typical man. I signaled my waiter, and told him to freshen our drinks. He nodded and scurried off to fill our order.

"Thank you," she said. "I'll tell him to put it on my tab when he returns."

"Don't worry about it, I got it," I said. "I know the owner. My name is Jackson." I extended my hand to her and was pleased by her softness as we shook.

"Nice to meet you, Jackson," she said. "My name is Nora."

# 29

# 11:59:51

If someone has never been in love, then they really have no idea of the lengths one will go to for their victim or oppressor. Sorry, my cynicism escaped right there. The falling in love is beautiful, the staying in love is rewarding, but the falling out of love is painful. How far would someone go for the person they're in love with? Would they give them their absolute last dollar? Would they vomit or become nauseous at the thought of their beloved with someone else? Would killing for them even be a thought? How about killing them? If the answer to more than one of those scenarios were absolutely "no," then one has never really been in love before.

Nora. Her name even sounded tasty as it left my lips.

"So what do you do while you sit here everyday, Nora?" I asked.

It was the first thing which came to my nervous mind. It had been a long time since I chatted up a woman, and my rustiness was apparent to me. I felt as if I had come off a little lame, but her response shocked me.

"I work my businesses, drink a few beers, and I sneak looks at you," Nora said. She smiled at me and right then, the game was over, decidedly in her favor. I felt myself blushing.

"Why didn't you say anything?" I asked. "I was trying not to be rude or forward, especially since I wanted you to keep coming back. It's my restaurant and I don't want to chase away customers just because I find them attractive." Pawn forward.

"Then maybe you need to take me somewhere else, so you can tell me about yourself," Nora said. Good countermeasure.

"Point taken. When? And where can I pick you up?"

"Let's meet somewhere. In case you don't like my company, you don't have to take me home," she said. "Here's my business card. You can send a text to my cell phone, and I'll answer promptly. Now, it's past time for me to go, but I thank you for finally saying something to me, Jackson."

When she rose, so did I. Nora shook my hand and walked away. The sway of her hips was hypnotizing, causing me to lose whatever thought had been in my mind. I couldn't wait until I saw her again.

A waiter hurried up to me, clutching the bill in his

hand. "Mr. Jackson, she didn't pay," he said.

I crumpled the bill up in my hand. "Don't worry about it," I said. "I'll take care of it."

I wanted to approach Nora differently than any man had ever approached her before. But since I wasn't picking her up, my options were limited. Then I had a brainstorm and I made a few phone calls.

The next day I sent her a text, telling her to meet me at Landry's that evening. It was a snazzy seafood restaurant down by the marina, which hopefully showed I had taste and class. A few minutes later, I received a text from Nora saying she would be glad to meet me there. While I had her business card in my hand, I perused it. According to her card, she made her living as a travel agent. Interesting, because I hadn't been anywhere new in a long time, and I was not averse to a vacation. Maybe she and I could plan a trip together in the near future. Yes, I was getting way ahead of myself.

I dressed in a cream linen short suit, with a matching pair of topsiders. I hoped she had never before experienced the type of date we were going to embark upon. I felt as if I had outdone myself.

I got to the restaurant early, right as the sun was beginning to head home for the evening. I let the valet park the Cadillac, and I took a few minutes to make sure all of my arrangements were in place. Twenty minutes later, a white convertible sports car pulled up with Nora at the wheel. I waved the valet off and I opened the door for her to exit. Nora was flawless in a white sundress and modest heels. Her appearance was classy, yet she was extremely sexy at the same time.

I helped her out of the convertible and hugged her briefly. I knew the price tag for the vehicle she was driving was upwards of 50,000 dollars, which made me think she was either doing very well as a travel agent, or came from a family with money. The valet handed me a ticket for her car, and then he zoomed away. Nora wore an oversized pair of sunglasses which completely hid her eyes, but her wide smile spoke volumes to me. It appeared as if she was as happy to see me as I was her.

"Our table won't be ready for a little while," I said." We can take a short walk, instead of us sitting at the bar, and being jostled by other patrons. Is that okay with you?

"That's fine with me, Jackson. I'm glad I didn't wear really high heels," Nora said. "For once, I couldn't think of what to wear, I was so nervous. I'm glad I kept it simple."

We walked toward the pier, and I tentatively reached for her hand. She put her hand inside of my arm, and we leisurely strolled towards the marina. The sails of the yachts swayed gently in the breeze, hypnotizing with their movements. I led her towards the boats, then I stopped, as a thought entered my mind which could ruin my plans.

"Do you get seasick?"

"Jackson, I grew up on airboats out on the bayous. I'm a Creole country girl, at home on land or water," she said. Her smile became brighter when I led her to a yacht where the captain was waiting for us.

"Shall we?" I asked.

She blushed and the captain led us onto the yacht. He tipped his hat to us once we were safely on board, and a crew member led us to the top deck, where we were seated at a small, round table. Our waiter popped a bottle of champagne and poured two flutes as soon as we were settled in our seats. The trio of musicians I'd hired were below deck, but the jazz they were playing could be heard clearly where we were seated.

As the captain eased the yacht out of its berth, I raised my flute to her. She raised hers in return, and I made a simple toast. "To new friendships," I said. The crystal made a tinkling musical sound as we clinked our glasses together. I fervently hoped this whole thing impressed her.

The yacht eased out onto Lake Pontchartrain, and for a change the water was calm and smooth. The breeze wafting over us was refreshing as we drank the champagne and watched the red sky becoming dark as the sun disappeared into the horizon. I refilled our flutes, pleased that the waiter was aware of my explicit instructions which had been, "Do not come out or to the table until I ring the bell." I wanted to get to know her without the intrusions of other people. I'd rented the yacht for the purpose of being alone, without the intimacy implied if we had dinner at my house.

"You're from here. I visited here as a teenager, and I've lived here since I graduated high school," I said. "Tell me your life story while we empty this bottle of champagne."

Nora laughed, and told me all about herself. Nora was the youngest and only girl. She was the baby and her brothers still treated her as such. She'd grown up in Lafourche Parish, was more than comfortable with country living, and she had spoken French all of her life.

She and I conversed in French then, which surprised and delighted her. I hadn't really used my linguistic skills since before Octavia had passed away. It was refreshing, as well as being a tremendous turn-on.

Nora was also from a mixed racial background, forging another bond between us. Her father was a dark-haired Cajun, and her mother was a Creole, who believed in saints and voodoo. She told me she embraced all parts of her cultural background, whereas I'd only been shown the darker parts of being biracial. As she talked, I'd ask questions periodically, but I could have listened to her mellifluous voice forever. She'd attended Xavier, and after graduation, she'd started a travel agency with money her brothers had invested in her. Her brothers had an import-export business, and she kept the books for them. She said she'd recently began dabbling in the stock market, but she acknowledged she was a novice. Nora didn't mention any past or current flames, and I knew better than to ask. There are some things a person never wants to know about a potential love interest.

In no time at all it seemed, we'd drunk two entire bottles of champagne. I rang the waiter and he served our dinner, which I'd had delivered by Landry's. I hadn't really misled her, because we did eat dinner from the restaurant. We dined on tender blackened catfish, spicy seafood jambalaya, and fresh French bread, which evened out some of the affects of the champagne. I needed it, because champagne serves as an aphrodisiac for me, which is why I rarely drink it. Over dinner I gave her an abridged history of my life, mentioning Tulane, my day trading expertise, and my sons. I didn't mention any of the dark shit which had happened in my life, because it was too soon for those types of intimate details.

After dinner, we drank an aged cognac while the musicians played smooth New Orleans jazz. I told Nora I hadn't dated in two years, and begged her patience, because I might be a little out of practice. We were standing by the rail of the deck, with the full moon serving as the only illumination for a moment I'd been imagining since the first time she stepped into my restaurant. I took Nora into my arms, and we swayed and danced to the music drifting over the deck. When the song ended, I paused in my movement, thrilled to be standing there holding Nora.

"You're doing fine so far," she said. Her lips parted slightly, and her eyes beckoned me closer. I leaned in and kissed her, intoxicated by the alcohol, the water, the moonlight, and her. She kissed me back, and I pulled her closer to me, feeling like the luckiest man in the world. Maybe I was.

# 30

# 11:59:53

The hidden parts of the human soul represent the scariest things imaginable. The soul is a mansion of rooms, with different architecture and blueprints for each person. The dark rooms of the human soul are filled with secrets, lies, imagined vengeance, buried passions, and the scars inflicted by life, which have never fully healed. It's almost impossible to glimpse the hidden darkness of a soul which is constantly veiled by a smiling visage.

I escorted Nora to her car after we left the yacht. Part of me was yearning to take her home with me, to taste the promise of her sumptuous body. I reflected on how my relationships had gone when I'd rushed to have sex in the past. They'd never worked out, because I had chased sexual intimacy too soon, without investing time in getting to know a romantic interest. I was determined to be strong-willed with Nora, to make this relationship different, because I felt as if I had finally met the one. Yes, the one, the woman my subconscious has dreamt of my entire life. The faceless woman I've always been convinced must exist, the one with the power to make all of my daydreams a reality. I'd finally met mine, and I wasn't going to sabotage it by pushing the sexual envelope.

I kissed her goodnight as I helped her into the convertible. She waved at me again as she drove off, making me wish I'd asked her to come back to my empty house with me. The valet opened my door, and I tipped him for his services. I'd never before been on a date like this, and I was proud of myself for how I'd planned it. Everything had gone wonderfully, and the money I'd spent was well worth it. I felt a bit tipsy, but not because of the alcohol. I was intoxicated by Nora Boudreaux, slightly drunk from the experience of my first date with her.

I pulled into my driveway and my phone rang. It was after midnight, so I immediately thought something was wrong with one of my kids. I heaved a sigh of relief when I recognized the number as Nora's.

"Is everything okay?" I asked.

"No, it's not," she replied. "What's your address?"

I slowly rattled off my address, then repeated it to her.

"Thanks," she said.

Then she hung up the phone. Puzzled, I looked at my

phone as I made my way to the door. Maybe she planned on sending me something the next day. Shrugging it off I went inside of my house and began to prepare myself for bed by taking my clothes off. I was walking up the stairs to the master bedroom, when I heard a knock at the front door. I hurried to the front door to see who could possibly be knocking this late. Clad only in my boxer shorts, I opened the door, and to my shocked and pleased surprise, Nora was standing on my doorstep, smiling at me. I opened the door and she came in. I closed the door behind her, then I turned to her, my expression both surprised and puzzled.

"I needed to taste you," she said. Her mouth was slightly open, and she licked her lips.

Nora fell to her knees in front of me, and I felt her soft hand easing into my boxer shorts. She withdrew my steadily lengthening manhood and smoothly inserted it into her cool, wet mouth. Her tongue circled my shaft, and she began to suck voraciously on my rock-hard shaft. In my shock, I sagged backwards, resting my back against the front door. Looking down upon her fast-moving head, I watched my shiny staff going in and out of her mouth. The simple act of observing her actions caused my heart rate to speed up and my stomach muscles to clench and tighten. It had been two years since my last sexual escapade and I was way overdue for a sexual release. As the warmth of her wet mouth engulfed me, I knew it wouldn't be long before I exploded. I weakly tried to push her away, but she was stronger than me right then. A whimper escaped from my throat, and less than two minutes later, I erupted into Nora's mouth. As she gamely swallowed it all, I was on the verge of passing out from this unexpected pleasure. With eyes closed, I felt her give a long, final suck, before she released my still throbbing dick from the prison of her mouth. I watched as she regained her feet, looking at me with the glazed look of a woman in lust. I tucked myself back into my underwear, then I stepped away from the door, ready to take her upstairs and make love to her for the rest of the night.

Nora stepped around me and opened the front door. I was bewildered because I couldn't fathom what she was doing.

"Thank you," she said. "I've been wanting to do that since we first met. I'll talk to you later."

Nora opened the front door, closing it softly behind her as she walked back to her crookedly parked convertible. I couldn't move to follow, because my knees were still weak from the force of the orgasm I'd experienced. I couldn't figure out what had just happened to me. I thought I was a good chess player, but Nora had bested me this round with a move I could not have prepared for.

Over the next few days, we had lunch together daily at Lee Jasper's. We sat together sipping flavored margaritas, and giving each other business tips. I instructed her on how to make consistent money on the stock market, giving her some of my practiced tricks and tips which I used to predict the longevity of a particular investment. Nora reciprocated by showing me how to gauge tech stocks. Was the market being glutted with products which all did the same thing? If so, then sell them and don't look back, because that market had already peaked. For a so-called novice, she was quick and savvy.

When she first began to day-trade under my tutelage, she'd started out with ten thousand dollars in her account. A person who can produce ten grand for a new business investment was someone worth knowing. After her first few days under my watchful tutelage, she'd tripled her initial investment. Nora had also convinced me to invest in products I normally would have bypassed. We'd only been dating a couple of weeks, and I'd already made a financial profit.

A funny thing happened between Nora and me, which tipped the scales of our relationship into new, unfamiliar territory. Over a pitcher of margaritas, I mentioned to her how I wanted my two boys to be brothers, not just by blood, but by familiarity. My casual mention of the hopes for my boys led to a revelation from Nora, which added to my belief she was the woman for me.

"As a girl, I couldn't understand why my father wasn't around very much," she said. "I didn't realize it then, but my two brothers and me were his outside children. He had a wife and five other children living less than five miles away from our little house. When I started going to school, I found out about the other Boudreaux children. There were five of them and three of us, and we all had the same features and the same last name. It was the biggest running joke in our parish, the many children of Benjy Boudreaux. We were called the "Wrong side of the blanket Boudreaux kids." It was humiliating, and it clung to us like mud. Our daddy acted like it was all okay, but my mother wept about our situation constantly. I didn't get away from the smirks, the sneers, and the jokes until I came to New Orleans for college. Now, I only go home for Thanksgiving and Christmas, which is a bit painful, as my father splits his time between two households. I vowed as a girl that I would never share a man with another woman."

Nora's story struck such a resonating chord within my soul, I found myself telling her about Lily, Flora Jean, Raymond, and Bobby Jr. Tears rolled down Nora's face while I told my story, especially the part about Flora Jean. I omitted any mention of money, and I only told her about my life up until the death of Octavia. Afterward, Nora rose from her chair, and came around to my side of the table, where sat on my lap and hugged me close to her. I could feel her heart beating next to mine, and it thrilled me because the pace and rhythm seemed as if we were sharing a single heartbeat.

I was at the point where I needed to see her every day, but we still hadn't slept with each other. It seemed as if we were both enjoying the newness of our relationship and did not want to ruin the courtship. We kissed often, joked constantly, and our flirtations could go from lightheartedness to heated in an instant. We also continued to make money together on a daily basis, while falling deeper into whatever it was we were falling into. I began to get a little nervous every time I saw her. My stomach would begin quivering and my mouth would go dry, as if the taste of Nora was the only thing which could satisfy my thirst. I'd never felt like this about anyone, not even Octavia. The dual feelings of fear and hope would descend whenever I heard her voice or knew I would see her. I didn't know what was happening to me until one day I was driving, listening to the radio. A song was playing, with the singer saying how a woman's love had changed his entire outlook on life. It was so profound, I had to pull the car over to the curb, where I reflected on this new relationship. I knew what malady I was suffering from. It had finally happened to me. I was falling in love for the first time in my life and I was scared as hell. What if Nora didn't love me the same way? What if I were the only one floating on this cloud? I didn't like this unfamiliar feeling of being powerless in a life situation. There was no chess move which could help me gain the upper hand in this relationship.

The afternoon when Nora's investment portfolio surpassed the $50,000 mark, she sat across from me at the restaurant and slid an envelope across the table. I was curious as to what could be inside, and when I opened it, my mouth fell open. Inside, there was a first-class plane ticket to Cozumel, Mexico. I looked at Nora in shock.

"Pack your bag and get ready," she said. "We leave Thursday, so I won't see you until then. You gave me the idea by telling me of your many trips with Octavia. I want to share those types of experiences with you and create new memories. I need you to imagine all we're going to do on this mini vacation, but I have to warn you, your imagination is going to fall short. I'll see you at the airport."

I was being beaten at my own game. Nora was playing me like a fiddle, and I have to admit I kind of loved it. I told both Susie and Dolores I would be out of the country for a few days, and to contact me if they needed me. I informed the general manager of Lee Jasper's of my imminent departure, and I readied myself for my vacation. Or at least I thought I was ready.

# 31

# 11:59:56

I know what some might be thinking right now. You're thinking it's been longer than a minute. Maybe. But not to me. My idea of the length of a minute must be different from yours, because if one really thinks about it, our lives are but a minute long in the grand scheme of the universe. That was a little bit deep, right?

I didn't see Nora when I boarded the plane for Mexico. I sat in my seat, while the coach passengers walked past me. Finally, she stepped onto the plane, her silky, curly hair in French braids. Her simple wraparound skirt and tank top showed off her curvy assets, causing lustful images to form of all the things I'd like to do to and with her. My mouth watered as I watched her walk toward me, and her red lips curved in a mischievous smile. She sat down next to me and buckled herself in. The kiss she gave me made my toes curl, as she sucked on my bottom lip before ending the kiss.

"Hold on," Nora said. "It gets a little rough from here." Truer words were never spoken.

Nora made good on her assurance to me about my imagination falling way short of the reality of us making love while we were in Mexico. The first time we made love occurred moments after we'd checked into our suite. Nora kissed me softly on my neck, running her lips and tongue along my ear. She licked my ear, and almost sent me over the edge by gently sucking my earlobe into her mouth. She unbuckled my linen shorts and used her soft hands to massage my member to a trembling state of hardness. Nora pushed me backwards onto the bed and removed my shorts. I pulled my shirt off and watched in amazement as she slowly removed her clothes, revealing inch after inch of her incredible body. She climbed on my prone body, and guided the course of our lovemaking session. I was a willing victim beneath her, letting her direct my hands and mouth where she wanted them. I submitted to her wants, needs, and demands until we came to a shaking, satisfying climax. I wondered at the enigmatic smile on her face in the aftermath of what may have possibly been the best sex of my life.

Afterward, Nora and I had drinks on the balcony, clad in the robes which the resort provided. Room service had brought us a pitcher of mango margaritas, which we sipped as we talked, with the full moon shining on us. I admitted to Nora how much I was looking forward to being the type of father to my children I'd wished for myself. Nora spoke of her daydreams of seeing the world with someone she loved and adored. Our conversation was more personal and intimate than any of our prior conversations and I almost spoke aloud the three words I was still too scared to say to myself. Maybe this was the beginning of a new chapter, where I would have someone to have and hold. Maybe this was also her first step on her journey to see the world with someone who adored her—me.

Later that night, we playfully kissed and petted in the shower which could have held four people. The heat between us erupted, and we feasted upon each other again, but I took control of our wet lovemaking. I had to attempt to regain the upper hand somehow. Our tryst in the shower came to a climax with my hand fisted in her curly hair and me pumping furiously in and out of her. I felt the convulsions of her multiple orgasms, and her moans and screams had reestablished my confidence. As we dried each other off afterward, I knew in my heart I was going down fast. If this were chess, it would be time to castle my king, because my king was in danger.

The next day Nora took me zip-lining, which was something I'd never even considered. It was a sensation of freedom and weightlessness which words can't describe. With the forest flying by beneath me, I realized spontaneity was an aphrodisiac, and I needed to indulge in being spontaneous a bit more in my carefully outlined life.

Sitting on the beach later, my ego received such a

huge boost from the reaction of the men on the beach at the sight of Nora in a bikini. I could understand their consternation, because my reaction may have been the same if she hadn't been with me. We lay on the beach, where we enjoyed eating freshly made tacos from a beachside cantina. We relaxed, sipping our frozen drinks, and talking of possible future vacations. I knew we'd have to experience something similar again soon, and we talked of different locales while the sun disappeared into the ocean.

I became feverish for her on our Mexican trip, not just because of the sex, but also because the companionship and laughter we shared was addictive. We had common interests, goals, not-so dissimilar backgrounds, and we had fun together. When we boarded our plane to return home we were holding hands, and I could not stop smiling. Happiness was a drug I could easily become addicted to, just as easily as I had fallen under Nora's spell.

Once we were back in New Orleans, the two of us became almost inseparable. Nora owned a townhouse in the French Quarter, but she was rarely there overnight. She spent most of her nights sleeping with me at my house, and I'd wake up smiling, intoxicated by the scent of her on my body and the taste of her still in my mouth. Heaven had finally found me, and hell was a distant memory.

I confessed my love to Nora five months after we'd started seeing each other. We were on the yacht where we had enjoyed our first date, but this time there was no band. There was only the captain guiding the boat, while we sipped wine beneath a lover's moon. I was definitely in unfamiliar territory, but the game was over as far as I was concerned. I was in love with her, and I loved her. There's a subtle difference between the two. Being in love with someone, one tends to overlook their flaws, such as snoring or rarely being on time. Loving someone, one is aware of all of their imperfections, but we love them despite their less than perfect ways. Nora wasn't perfect, but she was perfect for me. Nora cried when I uttered the three words I had never before told another woman.

"I love you," I said softly, looking into her eyes, while the tears slid down her cheeks. "Thank you for being in my life."

"I love you, too," she whispered, and our lips met in a soft and gentle kiss. It was the most beautiful night of my life. We were on to the next level of our relationship

A few days later, Nora arranged for me to meet her two brothers, Jacques and Pierre, who sized me up as we sat at a table at my restaurant. It was Jacques, the oldest one, who started questioning me.

"You love my sister?" he asked in his thick, Cajun accent. "Or is she just a plaything for you? Don't you already got kids from other playthings? Why is our sister any different?"

"Yes, I have two little boys, but they came because of one-night stands," I said. "I'm in love with your sister, and I hope to be with her forever. I take care of my sons, and I'll take care of your sister for the rest of my life, if she'll have me. I'm not going anywhere."

"You sound like you asking to marry her," Jacques

said. "Are you?"

"I guess I am," I replied with no hesitation. "I know your closeness, and I respect it."

The two brothers stared at me, then glanced at each other and shrugged their shoulders. They nodded at me and stood up, with their hands outstretched. I shook hands with them both, pleased at having received their blessing to marry their sister. They still seemed skeptical of me, but I couldn't blame them. If Nora had been my sister, I'd have been just as protective.

I still saw my two little boys monthly, and I was amazed at how quickly they grew. I was happy in all aspects of my life, and Nora was the cherry on top. I met with Susie when she dropped Liam off, and we sat on the porch swing companionably. I felt sheepish, but I needed to tell her my plans.

"I'm thinking of getting married to Nora," I said. "But I need to make sure my sons are set for life, because I might have more kids. I have the trusts set up, but I need to make sure they are untouchable and unbreakable."

Susie congratulated me, then assured me the trusts couldn't be touched by anyone, not even me. I thanked her profusely, hugging her and wishing her the kind of happiness I was enjoying. I made out my will that day with Susie, having her and the general manager of Lee Jasper's sign it as witnesses. I left Jasper the properties in Mississippi left to me by my mother and my grandmother, and Liam would receive the house in New Orleans. I named Dolores the executor of my will, because I knew Dolores would handle my business properly as she always had.

All of my legal stuff was out of the way, leaving me free to indulge myself in the pursuit of happiness with Nora Boudreaux. I was finally going to live the American Dream fully, with her at my side. I wouldn't propose to her until I felt the time was perfect, but I went and bought the engagement ring, a two carat, princess-cut diamond. I based the size of the ring on her shoe size, which according to experts, was the same size as a woman's ring finger. I would be prepared whenever the opportune time arose, and I couldn't wait much longer. Cloud nine was feeling fine, but I was ready for her to join me there.

Nora was extremely busy with her own affairs, so we weren't seeing as much of each other as I'd have liked. Her brothers were expanding their import business, and she was wrapped up with their affairs, making sure everything was handled correctly. Plus, she was thriving as both a day trader and as a travel agent. I wondered if she'd like to go to Bora Bora for our honeymoon, because it was one of her dream destinations. Thoughts like that ran through my mind at the oddest moments. It was an indication of how often I thought of her.

When she wasn't busy we'd eat dinner together, or maybe cuddle and watch television or a movie, and she'd spend the night at my house. The only time she didn't visit was if I had Liam or Jasper for the weekend. I'd asked her to meet them, but she was steadfast in her refusals, saying it was too soon to meet them. I shrugged it off because there'd be all the time in the world for her to meet my boys and to have a few more of my children. The possibilities for our future were boundless and I imagined buying a bigger vehicle, like a Suburban, so I could drive my tribe to Disneyland or the Grand Canyon.

The engagement ring was beginning to wear a hole in my pocket. I was ready to propose to her, but I needed her to be ready as well. I could be patient, because I'd been patient all of my life. Remember, I'm a chess player. The time and place needed to be perfect when I asked her to be my future everything.

One night Nora and I were sitting on her balcony, with the music of the Quarter providing the soundtrack for the frenzied lovemaking session we'd just completed. I decided it was finally the right time to ask her. I retrieved the ring from my pants pocket and slid the box into the pajama shorts I was wearing. She was clad only in a kimono, looking ravishing and ethereal. I crossed the short distance to where she stood, and I grabbed her hand.

I dropped to one knee and looked up at her, hoping the love I felt for her showed in my eyes. She was covering her mouth with her right hand, as if in shock. Her left hand was trembling in mine.

"I need you to know how much I love you, and the one thing I want most in this world is to spend the rest of my life with you," I said. "Will you marry me, Nora?"

"Oh my God!" she exclaimed. "Yes, yes, I will marry you!"

I slid the princess cut diamond ring on her finger and we stood on the balcony, where we hugged for what seemed like eons. The shirt I wore was damp from Nora's tears, and there were tears on my face as well. It had been a long time coming, but for the first time in my life, everything was perfect.

# 32

# 11:59:58

When a person has been single for a long time, they become set in their ways. They eat whenever they want to eat, sleep as long as they want to sleep, wherever they want to sleep, and a person has the freedom to come and go as they please. Living alone means there are certain things a person never does. They never lock their bedroom door, clothes are optional, they never worry about someone drinking their last beer, and they never lock their computer. What for? There's only one person to worry about and satisfy—themselves.

Nora and I started talking about what we wanted, as far as our wedding plans. I didn't care too much, because

I only had maybe six people to invite, without counting my employees. My children would have to be there, as well as their mothers, and Ms. Lenora, of course. It wasn't a big deal, and I felt those details were something we could work out later. Nora agreed, stating other than her immediate family she did not have many people to invite either. We discussed maybe having a destination wedding in Bora Bora or Aruba, or somewhere tropical. Money was no object, I admitted to her. Happiness has no price.

One morning, I had a craving for beignets. Nora was away for a couple of days, so I was alone. I hadn't had breakfast in the Quarter in so long, I figured I would enjoy a lazy day for a change. I dressed in shorts and a Tulane t-shirt, because I felt it would be the kind of day where I'd just bum around, maybe drinking by noon and listening to the music of the Quarter.

On my way to get the tasty sweets I grabbed a newspaper from a vendor, figuring I'd read it with my food. As usual, I'd been so caught up in my own life, I wasn't up to speed on the current affairs of the rest of the world. I figured I'd catch up with everything as I ate beignets. I ordered the hot, fluffy, powder sugared treats, plus a coffee and I grabbed a table. I thought to call my general manager to tell him I wouldn't be in when I realized it was his job to run the restaurant, I was just the owner. There was a reason I'd hired him, so I wouldn't have to constantly concern myself with the everyday operation anymore. I was on to my next project, which was marrying Nora

I opened my newspaper and began to read the latest

news. On page four, there was a picture of my father. Businessman and millionaire Robert Fitzgerald Jr. had died of a stroke the evening before. It went on to list his accomplishments, his birthday, and his next of kin. My name wasn't mentioned anywhere in the article.

I reached in my pocket for the phone, planning to call Susie and offer sympathy, but I didn't have it. In my mind, I retraced my steps from the night before and realized I must have left it in yesterday's pants. Shit. My phone call of condolences would have to wait.

I no longer had a taste for the food I'd craved only minutes before, and I pushed it away. I felt an overwhelming desire to have a drink right then, so I decided to go and have one or ten. He was dead, which eliminated any possibilities for a future reconciliation. There had always been a glimmer of hope in my soul I would one day have a decent and loving relationship with my father. I was suddenly depressed and with good reason. My father, nemesis, rival, and inspiration was gone. I say inspiration because all of my actions and achievements thus far in my life had been to make him proud of me—maybe even one day he'd have been proud enough of me to publicly acknowledge me as his son. Those daydreams were over now.

I think we eventually would have created some kind of cordial relationship, especially because of Jasper and Liam. I'm not such a hard-hearted man I would have denied him the chance and opportunity to get to know Jasper. He might have brought something good to that relationship, but now we would never find out. I know he'd been able to spend time with Liam, and I wonder how he felt about that. There would be no binding up of old wounds, or family barbecues at the Little League games, the things I'd secretly hoped would happen. Bobby Jr. was gone forever.

I walked through the Quarter rather aimlessly, I'm afraid. I stopped in a bar and sat down for a long while, with alcoholic drinks being the companion for my thoughts. Whatever illusions I'd had about maybe one day repairing the bridge with Bobby Jr. had been destroyed forever. He was gone, and we would never have a relationship as father and son, nor as friends. I toasted silently to him, asshole or not. I wouldn't be where I am or even exist, if it weren't for him. I hoped fervently he'd had an affection for me, even if he'd kept it to himself. I would call Susie and Liam once I had my phone again. I had to remind myself his death affected other people's lives as well.

I stumbled out of the bar an hour or so later, resuming my directionless walk through the Quarter. I stopped suddenly, needing desperately to talk to Nora. Fuck. Without my phone, I couldn't just call her, because her numbers weren't memorized. It wasn't like the old days before cell phones when we knew all the important numbers backward and forward. I rifled through my wallet and found her business card with her phone numbers and the address of her travel agency on it. I vaguely thought of using a pay phone to call her, when I had a realization. Funny, I'd never even been to her place of business and the address was only a couple of blocks away. Drunkenly, I couldn't remember if she'd told me whether she was back from her trip or not.

I bought a half dozen roses from a vendor on St. Peter's Street, just in case, then I walked toward the address. If she were back already, then my roses would be a welcome surprise. If not, I'd walk the blocks to her townhouse and leave the roses on her doorstep. Either way, she'd know I'd been thinking of her.

I reached the address, but I had to pull the business card out to verify I was at the right place. I compared and I was definitely in the right place. There was only one problem, though. The office was vacant, the windows were dusty, and it appeared to have been empty for quite a while. Interesting.

My mind started sobering up rapidly. I began to walk briskly, almost running to Nora's townhouse still carrying the six roses. Once there, it dawned on me I'd never come by on a whim, only when I was invited. The name on her mailbox didn't have the name Boudreaux on it. The name on the box read *Williams*. I dumped the roses in a nearby trashcan as ugly, unwelcome thoughts began overwhelming my brain.

I hailed a taxi and returned to my house, running through the door straight to my computer. I looked up the addresses for the office and the townhouse. The townhouse was owned by a Peter Williams, a name which rang no bells with me. The office owned by a real estate company and when I called them, I was informed the premises I was asking about hadn't been leased in the previous two years. After hanging up, I began researching Nora Boudreaux. I looked through birth records, alumni pages for Xavier University, and even the schools in Lafourche Parrish. Nothing. I couldn't find a single mention of her. It was as if there wasn't a person by the name of Nora Boudreaux. As if she didn't exist at all.

A sudden thought came to mind, and I switched my computer to my bank accounts. Of course my computer was not locked, I'd never locked it. I went through each bank file, with bile rising in my throat. Out of the more than six million dollars I'd had in various accounts, I barely had $400,000. Nora had cleaned me out. I threw up all over the computer, then I went looking for my phone. I had calls to make.

# 33

# 11:59:59

I ate about an hour ago. It was a pretty good meal but I've had much better in much swankier surroundings. Remember, I've eaten in some of the best restaurants in the world. The guards have been silently standing here for awhile, not saying anything to me, which is a blessing in itself. I'd told the priest to keep it moving when he'd shown up, because I'd be seeing God himself in less than four minutes, so I'd tell Him to His face what I had to say. Of course, I'd probably be going down instead of up, Dante's Inferno having assured me it would be so.

After cleaning the vomit off of my face, I'd called

Dolores, transferring $300,000 to her with the instructions to use it if I absolutely needed her to. She wanted to ask questions, but I still didn't know what answers I'd give her, so I hung up. I practiced breathing exercises for a few minutes, then I called Nora, or whatever her name was. She answered on the fourth ring.

"Hey baby!" I said. "Are you back from your trip?"

"Yeah, I got back a couple of hours ago," she replied. "What's up?"

"I just missed you, that's all. When can I see you?" I asked.

"You can come by my place later on, after seven—I should be there by then. I'm just tying up a few loose ends for my brothers," she said. "I'll be waiting."

We exchanged a couple more pleasantries, then we hung up. I knew where she'd be later, I just needed to get there ahead of time. In the back of my closet, there's an old shoe box. Inside the shoebox is my nine-millimeter handgun, plus two boxes of ammunition. I'd learned how to shoot as a teenager when Bobby Jr. sent me to a western camp for a summer vacation. *Maybe I wouldn't have to pull it out,* I thought, as I tucked it into my waistband.

I put my gun in the glove box of the Cadillac, then I drove back to the townhouse. Since she'd said she'd be home around seven, I'd have time to search the townhouse before she got there. I parked the Cadillac a couple of blocks away, in a paid parking lot where Nora couldn't possibly run across it. I walked around the back of the townhouse, then I picked the lock on the back window with a screwdriver and I was in. I laid the screwdriver on the kitchen counter, and I began exploring the house.

It was decorated exactly as I remembered it. I started looking around. I opened up all of the closets, cabinets, shoe boxes, and even went through the kitchen drawers. I didn't find anything which could have been helpful with my quest. There were no documents or anything else which could identify Nora or lead me to the recovery of the money which she had stolen. I slowly and methodically looked around the place once more. There weren't even any pictures of anyone on the walls, and I couldn't remember if there ever had been. It was a sterile and anonymous living space.

I was standing in the living room, feeling dumbfounded, when I heard multiple voices approaching the front door. Quickly, I stepped into the front closet, pulling the door closed behind me. I hoped I hadn't left any traces of my search, but if so, oh well. It was time to find out the truth anyway.

The front door opened, and the conversation being held became clear and audible. It was Nora, plus two men, her brothers. But were they even that? Was her whole life a preconceived fabrication? The undeniable truth rocked my soul to the core, while just like my feelings for my father, there was the faintest hope I could be wrong about everything. Her next words confirmed my heartbreak.

"He's supposed to come by here tonight," Nora said. "But I'll call him in a little while with some excuse as to why I can't see him. I'll need the head start, but I plan to be somewhere else and someone else by tomorrow."

Male laughter followed her statement. I couldn't believe what I was overhearing. This was too much.

"But you kind of liked him, didn't you bébé?" a male voice said. I identified it as one of her brothers, the one she'd introduced to me as Jacques. "Otherwise you'd have taken everything, as you usually do."

"He is actually a pretty nice guy, but he's just another mark," Nora said. "He's smart enough to build his fortune back up with what we left him, so he'll be fine. We've transferred all of the money to different accounts, so he won't be able to trace it. This was a huge score, so I think we're done after this one. Tomorrow at this time, I'll be in the Cayman Islands picking up my money. We each get a million dollars, and I have your shares in cash in the back of my car. Good job fellas."

A million a piece? They'd stolen six million, and she was still going to cheat her own partners. Whoever this woman was, she was truly ruthless and cared for no one but herself. I'd been hoping for something redemptive to come out of her mouth, but I was mistaken again. I'd been mistaken about everything regarding the person I'd known as Nora Boudreaux.

*When the Saints go Marching In* suddenly started playing, because I had neglected to turn my cell phone off. I hit the mute button, but it was too late. The closet door was snatched open, and a huge fist hit me in the face. I tried to fight back, but that first punch had knocked me silly. Jacques and Pierre were too much for me, and I knew there was no chance I could beat the two burly men. They thoroughly beat my ass, while Nora just stood there and watched the action. I was pummeled back and forth for what seemed like hours to me, but was in reality only about two minutes. There's the funny thing about time again, right?

I somehow managed not to black out, and I kept moving, causing some of the blows which could have knocked me out to glance off my arms, head, or shoulders. I fell to the ground once, but I rolled a few feet, then popped up before they could start kicking me with their steel-toed work boots. I managed to duck a roundhouse punch from Pierre, then I hit him with a quick jab, and bolted out the front door.

I ran like a wounded deer the two blocks to my car. They hadn't given chase, meaning they weren't too worried about me calling the police or anyone else. I never even thought of calling the police. My body wasn't aching at that point, even though I knew it would later. I unlocked the Cadillac, and retrieved the gun I'd left in it. My only thought as I put the nine-millimeter into my waistband was that my king was in check, and the game was almost over. I walked quickly back toward the townhouse, with blood streaming down my face. I knew my nose was broken, but it wasn't important to me at that moment. I could still recover two million dollars of my money if I hurried and didn't waver in my actions.

It wasn't just the money, though. It was everything which had ever happened to me. It was the smell of Flora Jean's blood in the air, the sneer on the face of Lars Jr., the memory of always being an outcast, and the rage I felt overtook any fear I may have had. I'd worked and suffered too much already, and I was not going to let them take my money off into the clear blue yonder. Fuck that. I would do what I needed to do, and God help them.

Her car was still parked in the front of the townhouse, meaning they hadn't left. Good. I ran silently around the back and quietly entered the townhouse through the still open window. I walked slowly and silently towards the living doom, where their raised voices covered any small sounds I may have made.

The three of them were standing in the living room where I had left them, and I felt my rage becoming an icy coolness.

"We can't leave yet," Nora said. "There are a few things I need to take care of, but we can be gone in the next couple of hours. It's not a problem."

*Yes, it was a problem*, I thought. What things could she possibly need to take care of? *It didn't matter*, I thought, as my gun hand raised of its own accord. It didn't matter at all. Pointing a gun is as simple as pointing one's finger and squeezing the trigger, not jerking it. If you practice enough, you'll always hit the target. I used my left hand to steady my right one for the recoil, and I aimed, squeezed, shifted the barrel slightly to the left, aimed, and squeezed the trigger again.

Night, night fellas, as the two quick head shots put Jacques and Pierre out of their misery. Their heads hadn't exploded as Raymond's had, but the blood spatter and pieces of brain matter were everywhere, even on Nora. Her two-piece cream linen suit was ruined. I almost smiled.

I trained the gun on her shocked face, but I didn't squeeze the trigger then. I should have, but I needed answers. I motioned her away from the two bodies sprawled on the living room floor, and I directed her to sit in the chair behind the desk. I knew I didn't have long to do what I needed, because time was slipping away from me. She was still so fucking beautiful to me.

"Why me?" I asked, walking closer to the desk. "You picked me, didn't you?"

"Why not you?" she replied. "When you opened your restaurant, there was a feature on you in the newspaper. I researched you enough to know you had plenty of money. We formulated our plan and I put myself in your life."

I moved closer to her, my fingers itching to squeeze the trigger. I lowered the gun. I motioned to the two bodies lying on the floor. "Who were they?" I asked. "And who are you?"

"Jack and Pierre were two guys I grew up with on the bayou," she said. "We've been friends, lovers, and partners in crime since we were teenagers. I'm Noreen Bouchard."

"Open your laptop," I said. "I'm giving you the chance to make things right."

She opened her laptop, and then her gaze returned to me. She was shocked, but she didn't look scared at all. She should have been.

"Put the money back. Transfer it now, and your chance of living beyond the next few minutes might improve," I said.

"I don't know your routing number."

"I do."

I rattled off the numbers I'd memorized long ago, and her slim fingers tapped on the keyboard. She hit the "enter" key, then turned the laptop so I could see the screen. It was done.

"Was it all part of the act?" I asked her. "Did you feel anything for me? Anything at all?"

"No," she replied. "I felt absolutely nothing for you."

I took a step closer to the desk, easing next to the side of it, and without breaking eye contact, I fingered the paperweight sitting on the desk. It was a heavy, miniature globe of the world. My fingers wrapped around it, and I hit her with the world with as much force as the world had beaten me. The blood shot out of her nose where I had hit her, and her face whipped to the side from the force of the blow.

"Nice to meet you, Noreen," I said, and I felt the devil rise within me. I smashed her in the face with the world, and all of the past hurts and heartbreaks echoed in the blows I rained down upon her formerly beautiful face. I couldn't hear the screams coming out of my soul, and all thoughts of anything else were gone from my mind. I was still striking her dead body, beating her face unrecognizable, when the police pulled me off her.

Checkmate.

# 34

# 12:00:00

I sat in the police station afterward, in a small room with two uniformed cops and a couple of detectives. Every time they fired a question at me, I answered with the same two words—"phone call." Finally, one of the detectives grabbed my arm, and I stood and followed him out of the room. He stopped at a desk, and motioned me to sit. He picked up the phone and looked at me.

"What's the number?"

I recited Dolores's cell number and he dialed, then put the receiver to his ear. I heard her say "Hello," and he handed me the phone. He walked away a few feet, giving me a small bit of privacy.

"Hey, it's me," I said. "Don't talk, just listen. Contact a defense lawyer, because I need one. Also, you're in charge of my offshore accounts. You know what to do. I'm under arrest."

"I got it," she replied. "Should I bring a checkbook when you're arraigned?"

"No, don't even bother. There's no bail when the charge is murder."

I was arraigned the next morning, where I was charged with three counts of first-degree murder, unlawful use of a firearm, and twelve more charges. Dolores was there, and I wouldn't allow myself to stare at her. It was obvious I'd made the wrong choice in my love life. I learned Jack and Pierre Bonet really had been brothers, and I wondered if Noreen had slept with both of them, or only one of them. Probably both, but what did it matter? I almost laughed as my expensive lawyer argued that bail should be considered. The judge shut him down rather quickly, and twenty minutes after the arraignment, I was escorted in a police van to the county jail.

I was in a cell with two other men, and even though they peppered me with questions, I had nothing to say to them. They were both smaller than me, and I didn't feel as if I were in any danger from them. I found out rather quickly that I was in harm's way whenever I was out of the cell. The Bonet brothers seemed to have had a lot of friends and relatives.

I received a lot of menacing looks and stares from other inmates, but I felt no fear. I was beyond it. I thought it would just be dirty looks and jeering insults, as it had been at Boniface. I didn't think anyone would have the balls to try anything physical, as I towered over most of the other inmates. It didn't take long to realize I had misjudged the situation. But they had also misjudged me.

A fight broke out between two men on the other side of the cafeteria, and the guards ran over to break it up. Some sixth sense kicked in for me, and I managed to dodge the thrusting arm of a smaller guy who was attempting to kill me with a sharpened toothbrush. I grabbed his arm with my left hand, and with my right, I grabbed him around his throat. I pushed him against one of the tables, using it as an aid as I choked the man to death. I let his limp body fall to the floor, with his tongue protruding and his eyes bulging. Unfortunately for me, two guards saw me kill the guy. Manslaughter and assault were added to my charges. My grim situation became even more so, and I spent the rest of my time at the county jail in solitary confinement. It didn't bother me one bit.

As I lay on the hard cot in the darkness, I thought of the choices I'd made. I thought of all the things I'd seen and done, and by the time my trial date arrived, I was resolute as to how I would proceed with what remained of my life.

My lawyer entered a plea of "Not Guilty," but he and I both knew I was guilty as charged. He'd tried to convince me to seek a plea agreement, but I was having none of it. I probably could have only received life if I'd shot her when I shot the Bonet brothers. If I'd taken the gun into the townhouse with me the first time, I might have gotten away with three counts of manslaughter or something much less than what I was eventually charged with. I'd been unprepared. Once I went back to my car to retrieve my pistol, the prosecutor successfully argued everything which followed became premeditated. I hadn't been as prepared as a good chess player should always be.

The prosecutor had his eye on higher office, so there was no plea deal offered. He wanted to make an example of me for his future constituency, and I knew what the outcome would be. My lawyer did his best to put on some kind of a defense, talking of the robbery and fraud committed against me, but it was useless. The financial crimes committed against me by the trio wasn't enough to justify me shooting the Bonet brothers, or the twenty-seven times I'd struck Noreen with the globe paperweight. My lawyer implored me to at least try an insanity plea, so maybe I'd only receive a life sentence with no possible chance for parole. I refused, because I still remembered the cells I'd seen at Alcatraz. I wouldn't live the rest of my life in a cage like an animal, no matter what else I was facing.

The pictures of the murder scene were shown during the trial, causing gasps and outrage from the assembled onlookers. When the lawyers finished their closing arguments, it took the jury all of forty-seven minutes to convict me on all charges. My story hadn't meant a thing to them, especially after they'd been bombarded with the before-and-after pictures of Noreen's face. I'd been convicted by a jury of my peers, some who probably had far worse life stories than me. The difference being they hadn't murdered three people, no matter how bleak their existence had been.

The judge gave me the death sentence like he was

doing me a favor, which I guess he was. I didn't even blink, because I'd already been dead inside ever since I'd discovered Nora was an illusion.

# 35

# 12:01:01

The two million dollars in cash, which had been in the trunk, was returned to my estate, after much debate and investigation. It didn't matter too much, because when murder is committed by a person of means, there will always be civil suits filed by relatives or spouses. The two million would be split up amongst vultures, but they wouldn't be able to touch any of the other money I'd hidden away.

Dolores promised she would make sure my sons received their inheritance. I told her and Susie everything which had happened, and they implored me to fight the sentence I'd been given. It wasn't even in me to fight anymore, I told them. Life had won, and I was ready to go—exit stage left. I asked the mothers of my children to give them the truth about me when they turned eighteen, as part of their inheritance. I wanted them to know who I had been in my short life, and that I had been much more than a murderer, which would be the title society would use to label me.

I never appealed the conviction, nor did I ever attempt to delay it, so here I am, two short years later, walking toward my destiny. I knew a crowd would be waiting to see the event, and some of the onlookers would be happy at my fate, but I no longer cared. Honestly, I'm apathetic about this whole thing, with my only trace of sadness or regret being I won't physically be here to see my boys grow up. I would have been a great daddy. I would have taken them fishing often, or to watch baseball games. Later, I would have taught them to drive, and shave, and knot a necktie, and all of the other things a daddy should want to do with his kids. Despite my best wishes, though, they'd be deprived of a father, just as I had, through no fault of their own.

I was strapped onto the table, and my limbs were shackled into place. I wasn't scared at all, because I was ready for this life to be over. I heard someone reading the charges I'd been convicted of, but I'd already closed my eyes. The beautiful faces of my sons, Flora Jean's sweet laugh, Lily's scent, the redness of Octavia's hair, the ceiling of the Sistine Chapel, and dozens of other beautiful memories flooded my mind. I had made the most out of my existence, I guess, but I was more than ready to leave this thing called life. Shakespeare flits into my mind. "Life is a tale told by an idiot, full of sound and fury, signifying nothing." Brother, ain't that the truth?

As the realization hit me that my life was almost over, I understood everything that happened to me, and the motivation for all I had done. The answer was simple, and I wish I'd known much earlier in my life. Maybe things would have been different.

Love. It makes the world go around, and it gives meaning to the human existence. I had suffered from the lack of it, sacrificed for the need for it, begged for any semblance of it, and my quest for love was the reason for everything.

A voice asked me if I had any last words or statements to say.

"I hope the fish are biting," I said.

I envision Lily, Flora Jean, and Octavia waiting for me. Laughter and music, surrounded by people who had genuinely loved me. I smell magnolia blossoms and honeysuckle, wishing I was fishing right now. In my head, a brass band starts playing *I'll Fly Away*. The taste of gumbo is on my lips, and I smile happily, as the needle is plunged in.

# ACKNOWLEDGEMENTS

I'd like to thank my original beta readers, Carla Ray Henson and Sherri Malarkey for their feedback and support with this project and others. Also, shout-out to my team, Tasha Morris, Venessa McDaniel Cerasale, and my editor, Gordon Bonnet. We did it. Teamwork makes the dream work.

Keep reading for a sneak-peek of the prequel to *11:59*:

## *Singing to Butterflies*

Coming August, 2023 from
Marlon Hayes and Motina Books.

# Singing To Butterflies
## Chapter One
## Flora-Jean

On pretty afternoons I sat at the little creek behind our house. Under the shade of a huge cypress tree, I devoured books about other people, other places, and other times. My momma, Lily, called me every once in a while, making sure I hadn't fallen asleep too close to the water. It only happened once, but ever since, she wasn't taking any chances. I was her only child, and my momma made sure I knew my position.

"Flora Jean, quit running so much! This Mississippi heat will make you pass out, and you my only child! I ain't got no replacement for you!" "Flora Jean, get away from the edge of the water! You my only child, so you be't not drown!" For every situation in my young life, my momma let me know how precious I was to her. Sometimes I likened our relationship to an owner and a prized mule, but in my momma's eyes, ours was the kinship between a queen and a queen-in-training.

Momma let me spend hours outside reading my books without interfering too much. The radio which sat just inside our kitchen played the blues, and she turned the volume up enough for me to hear the music down by the creek. Most afternoons she brought me out fried chicken, fish, or other home cooked food to snack on. She quietly tapped me on the shoulder, handed me a plate, then disappeared back into the house or to our small barn. My momma didn't begrudge my reading time as wasteful like a lot of other parents did. She knew I daydreamed of leaving here for college and the world beyond, and she was dreaming right along with me.

When you are twelve going on thirteen, it seems as if anything is possible in this life, even in rural Mississippi, where we lived in a small house not too far from a small town. I thought everything was small because all of the things I read about were huge, jaw-dropping stuff I could only imagine. Subways, airplanes, skyscrapers, and ocean liners were just some of the things which I couldn't witness for myself due to where we lived. In Mississippi, there were only a couple of ways to get around—by car or on foot. Walking country roads was not advisable for a young Black girl, because things could happen. One day I'd get away from Mississippi, and I would only come back once a year to see my momma.

My life was simple because my momma made it that way. We really weren't farmers, so I didn't toil in the fields or anything like that. We had a pretty huge garden though, and a whole bunch of chickens. I gathered eggs in the mornings from the coops, sprinkled corn amongst the chickens, washed the eggs off, and that was it, as far as morning chores. Once cleaned, Lily might sell a couple of dozen eggs down at the market for "pin money," but we weren't really selling eggs or chickens to get by, something I learned before I was ten.

At school, I was regarded by my classmates as some-one special, I guess. No one ever bullied me or ridiculed the way I liked to answer as many of the questions from the teacher as I could. At recess I ran with and from the boys, or I jumped rope with the girls. Sometimes, when the mood was on me, I sang to the butterflies. All it took was for a big old monarch to alight somewhere near where I was playing, and the rest of the world vanished while I sang odes to butterflies.

I always sang, whether I was happy, sad, upset, whatever. Singing to butterflies kind of just happened one day while I was reading a book by the creek, humming a hymn which I was practicing for church. A butterfly landed on a bush three feet from where I was sitting. The slow, rhythmic flapping of its wings was like a song of their own, and words came from my mouth in harmony with the melodic movements of its wings. I timed my words, changing the tone of my voice, singing a sweet song to a beautiful creature which seemed to respond. It fluttered, seeming to be dancing to my song, and when I hit the high note ending the song, the butterfly rose towards the sky, as if my song had renewed its spirit. From then on, whenever a butterfly flew near, or rested close by, I sang a song to it.

Of course people remarked on my behavior, talking about the girl who sang to butterflies. No one ridiculed me or called me crazy, but I felt different from everyone, as if I had been given a gift from God which let butterflies dance to the sound of my voice.

# ABOUT THE AUTHOR

Marlon S. Hayes is a writer from Chicago, Illinois, who loves his family, his three dogs (even Polly!), his friends, traveling, cooking, and the Chicago Cubs.

Made in the USA
Monee, IL
26 August 2022